PENGUIN CRIME FICTION

DEATH OF A DUTCHMAN

Magdalen Nabb has lived in Florence since 1975. Her first book, *Death of an Englishman* (also available from Penguin Books), was published to widespread critical praise. Originally a potter, she now writes full-time and is working on a third crime novel, which, like her first two books, is set in Florence.

DEATH OF A DUTCHMAN

MAGDALEN NABB

PENGUIN BOOKS

Penguin Books Ltd, Harmondsworth,
Middlesex, England
Penguin Books, 40 West 23rd Street,
New York, New York 10010, U.S.A.
Penguin Books Australia Ltd, Ringwood,
Victoria, Australia
Penguin Books Canada Limited, 2801 John Street,
Markham, Ontario, Canada L3R 1B4
Penguin Books (N.Z.) Ltd, 182–190 Wairau Road,
Auckland 10, New Zealand

First published in the United States of America by
Charles Scribner's Sons 1983
Published in Penguin Books 1984

LIBRARY OF CONGRESS CATALOGING IN PUBLICATION DATA
Nabb, Magdalen, 1947–
Death of a Dutchman.
I. Title.
[PR6064.A18D38 1984] 823'.914 83-25023
ISBN 0 14 00.6935 6

Printed in the United States of America by
George Banta Co., Inc., Harrisonburg, Virginia
Set in Baskerville

DEATH OF A
DUTCHMAN

CHAPTER 1

'Signora Giusti!' protested Lorenzini, holding the receiver away from his ear and throwing open his free hand in despair. Across the room, the plump, pink-faced carabiniere who had been about to roll a fresh sheet of paper in to the typewriter stopped and grinned. He could hear everything that the chattering voice on the other end of the line was saying from where he sat, and when it stopped he was still grinning.

'That's twice today and three times yesterday,' he said.

'Oi-oi-oi!' grumbled Lorenzini, replacing the receiver with a grimace. But he added, 'Poor old biddy.'

Last time she'd got him round there she had kept him for most of the morning, telling him the story of her life, interrupting herself each time he got up to leave to invent some new complaint against one or other of her neighbours. The Florentines hated her, she claimed, because she was Milanese. As she recounted the persecution she had to suffer, huge tears rolled down her face and splashed on to her tiny hands which were as thin and pale as a sparrow's legs.

'And I'm ninety-one years old!' she would wail pitifully. 'Ninety-one years old . . . I'd be better off dead . . .'

'No, no, Signora, come on, now.' And each time the unfortunate young man sat down on the edge of a hard chair and tried to quiet her, off she would go again about the quarrel that had broken out over her engagement — seventy-three years ago but it seemed like yesterday! — and the tiny hands would gesticulate happily, the moist eyes glitter with malicious delight at having recaptured her victim.

'Do you want me to go?' the pink-faced carabiniere

asked, starting to get up.

'I don't think you'd better, you'd never cope. I'll tell the Marshal—is he still downstairs?'

'Yes . . . at least, he was still struggling with that American couple when I came up.'

Lorenzini rolled down his sleeves and reached for his khaki hat.

'I'll have to go round there, I suppose . . .' He glanced at his watch. 'It's going on for twelve, anyway. I'll take the van and pick up the lunches. Ciao, Ciccio.'

Ciccio's real name was Claut, Gino Claut, but in Florence nobody ever called him by his real name, perhaps because it sounded German. He had dozens of nicknames: Gigi, Ciccio, for his plumpness, Polenta—either because he came from the north or because his cropped yellow hair was the colour of polenta, the maize flour they eat up there—and Pinocchio, for no particular reason, although his shiny, smiling face and slow movements were a bit puppet-like. His uniform never seemed to encompass all of him no matter how he adjusted it, and a corner of his shirt collar was usually sticking up awkwardly against his pink chin. He had enlisted with his brother who was a year older and looked just like him except for being a bit taller and slimmer, and together they were known as "the boys from Pordenone", always with an accompanying smile. In fact, they didn't come from Pordenone itself but from a tiny village twenty kilometres to the north, right at the foot of the Dolomites. Gino liked all his nicknames. His smile got wider and his face pinker the more the other lads teased him. He smiled now as Lorenzini clattered down the stairs. Lorenzini always clattered everywhere, always in a rush. Then a look of wide-eyed concentration settled on his face as he stuck his tongue out at one corner of his mouth and began to type slowly with two stubby fingers.

Downstairs, in the small front office, Marshal

Guarnaccia's broad expanse of back entirely blocked the grille through which the Americans were making their complaint. A patch of sweat had soaked through his khaki shirt between the shoulders, and every now and then he stopped to run a handkerchief round his neck. First he'd had to explain to them, in sign language and Italian words of one syllable to which they made no effort to listen, that they must go to a tobacconist and buy a sheet of *carta bollata*, the government stamped paper on which all official communications have to be written. When they finally got back with it, sweating and furious after having quarrelled with three bar owners who didn't have a stamp and tobacco licence, he'd had to write it out for them, laboriously eliciting each morsel of information by more sign language. Now, an hour later, they had reached the description of the stolen Instamatic camera, only to announce that it had been stolen the day before in Pisa. The Marshal, red in the face, put his pen down and turned away, glad to be interrupted by Lorenzini.

'What is it?'

'Signora Giusti, Marshal.'

'Again?'

But it was always like that; sometimes they heard nothing from her for six or seven months, then the calls would start coming in every day. Once she had telephoned six times in one day, and always with a plausible story. Nevertheless, if once they failed to check and then something happened to her, the newspapers would have a field day; "Ninety-one-year-old woman dies alone after SOS call ignored."

'Shall I go round there?'

'You'd better, I suppose — no, wait. You can speak a bit of English, can't you?'

'A bit. Not properly, but enough to deal with them . . .'

'In that case, try and explain to them that they should have denounced the theft in Pisa. They've had me pinned here all morning and I still haven't checked the hotels. I'll call on Signora Giusti myself on the way back . . .'

He buttoned himself into his jacket hurriedly and took his hat from the hook as he went out the door. He was a little ashamed at leaving the lad to cope—they would be furious now at having been palmed off with a sub-ordinate—still, if he knew a few words of English, that might help to quiet them. But when he paused under the big iron lamp of the stone archway to put on his sun-glasses he could hear the American's voice clearly:

'Because we were just there for the day! Why should we use up the bit of time we had there! We're staying right here just across the way—listen, I can't see why you should waste our whole morning like this!' And all the time the woman's voice lamenting uncertainly in the background, 'Maybe I did leave it on the bus, after all . . .'

Even without understanding a word the Marshal shook his head at the hopelessness of it all.

It was July, and the sloping forecourt in front of the Pitti Palace was filled with brightly-coloured coaches, the hot air shimmering above them. To make your way down among them would bring your blood to boiling point. The Marshal walked across in front of the palace where the postcard-sellers had their stalls and a man with a cart sold ice-cream that began to melt sloppily before the customer had even paid for it. He saw two Japanese girls walking away from the ice-cream man, licking their cones and talking rapidly, and paused to tap one of them on the shoulder. They both turned to stare up at the fat military man in black glasses who silently handed them the guide book they had left on the edge of the cart.

No doubt, he thought uncharitably as he went on his way, they'd have decided it was stolen and gone to Milan to denounce it.

He made his way down the slope at the far end of the forecourt where the high stone wall offered a little shade, and crossed the narrow road, threading his way through a stationary queue of cars. Some of the drivers were hooting and groaning in a desultory manner but it was too stickily hot for them to bother getting out to argue.

The Marshal walked slowly from hotel to hotel, his hands dangling at a distance from his body like the over-weight hero of a Western, glancing unobtrusively into each parked car he passed, glancing for a split second longer into those that didn't have Florentine number plates. Every day except Thursday, which was his day off, he checked the blue police registers of every hotel and pensione in his district against a list of wanted terrorists supplied to all the police forces by *Digos*, the secret police. He wasn't obliged to do it, and he knew well enough that terrorist operations were conducted from private houses, but he did it just the same. Sometimes it got results because if it was just a case of a meeting or a long journey they did use hotels, and if they used the ones in his quarter the Marshal wanted to be the first to know about it. It wasn't a personal vendetta but he had his own private reasons. Terrorism was to him a middle-class phenomenon which he didn't consider himself competent to understand. He understood people who were just trying to keep their heads above water and who resorted to thieving and prostitution to do it, and those who gave up and went begging on the Via Tornabuoni. Young ones, too, who gave up before they started. Crossing Piazza Santo Spirito to his last call before lunch, he saw two of them slumped on a bench under the dappled shade of the trees. The boy seemed to be asleep, the girl listlessly watching a trickle of dark blood roll down her forearm. A dirty hypodermic, a teaspoon and half a squeezed lemon lay on the ground beside the bench.

' 'Morning, Marshal.' The proprietor of the Pensione Giulia was downstairs at the main entrance in his shirt-sleeves, watching the Marshal pick his way through the squashed fruit and pecking pigeons that surrounded the scattering of market stalls along one side of the square.

'Nobody new since yesterday,' he added hopefully.

'I'll come up just the same,' said the Marshal blandly, quite unperturbed by the unpopularity of his little calls. The pensione was on the third floor.

'This one here—' the Marshal's plump finger pointed to the last name on the register—'wasn't here yesterday.'

'Yesterday, no . . . it's someone who was here . . . must have been a month ago . . . went off on a tour and asked me to save the same room—well, I wouldn't want to waste your time on somebody you'd already checked a month ago . . .'

'A month ago?'

'I could be wrong . . . or, of course, it might have been a Thursday when you don't—'

'A Thursday?'

'I'd have to check . . .'

'Check.'

The proprietor was fiddling nervously through the register when a door behind him opened and a jaunty little man in a crumpled blue linen suit came out. He stopped dead when he saw the visitor but then sauntered forward with his hands in his pockets.

'Looking for someone, Marshal?' he chirped brightly.

The Marshal considered him for a moment and then said, 'You.'

The little man turned furiously on the proprietor.

'You cretin! You said you wouldn't let him in!'

'And you promised to stay in your room! It's not me who's a cretin!' The little man turned to the Marshal who was watching them both with expressionless, bulging eyes while telephoning to Borgo Ognissanti headquarters for a car.

'I only had six months left to do, d'you know that? Six months! I might as well have stayed inside . . .'

The Marshal said nothing.

When the car arrived and three carabinieri thundered up the stairs, he said:

'No panic, lads. Just one harmless chap.'

They looked at the Marshal and then at the little man.

'Who is he?'

'I've no idea. Even so, he says he's still got six months of a sentence to serve, and he doesn't seem to have signed the register.'

'Come on, come on!'

The little man was struggling and swearing violently as they tried to remove him.

'What the devil's the matter with you? Let's go!'

'He's annoyed,' the Marshal said, 'about having told me. He seemed to think I knew who he was.'

'All egoists,' one of the lads remarked as they finally got their man out the door.

'Yes,' sighed the Marshal, considering his little trick rather ashamedly, 'I suppose we are.'

Then he turned, leaned heavily with his big fists on the reception desk and stared so long and so hard at the proprietor that his great eyes seemed about to bulge right out of his head.

'You were saying? This person booked in a month ago?'

'Last night,' the proprietor corrected himself, much subdued.

'Nothing to do with our escapee friend, I take it?'

'No, no. Just a tourist. I just didn't want you to come up . . .'

'Of course you didn't. But one of these days—' the Marshal looked up and wagged a finger—'you'll be shouting for help and then you'll expect me to come running.'

His finger went back to the new registration.

'British passport . . . why haven't you recorded the date of issue?'

'Haven't I? I must have forgotten . . .'

'Was it out of date?' The Marshal was leaning towards him so that they were almost nose to nose.

'No, of course not. I expect I've jotted it down somewhere . . .'

'In that case you'll find it for when I call tomorrow.'

The Marshal copied the name Simmons and the passport number into his notebook to remind himself.

'One of these days . . .' he warned the proprietor again.

'It was only for a night, Marshal. No harm done.'

Out in the piazza the market traders were packing up amid a strong scent of basil and big ripe tomatoes, the smell of summer. There were only a few stalls because it was Monday morning. The artisans' workshops were closed for the same reason and only the bar, with its white-painted iron tables outside, was open and busy with the tourists.

The rest of the piazza was rapidly emptying, and new smells were starting to filter out between the slats of the brown persian shutters, all closed now against the midday sun; smells of roasting meat, garlic, herbs and frying olive oil. The Marshal noticed he was hungry. The last stall in the line still had one tray on the end of it with a dozen or so huge, furry peaches packed in fresh grass.

'One thousand five a kilo,' said the stall-holder in the large green apron, catching his glance and reaching for a brown paper bag. 'Here you are, two thousand the lot, and let's get home to our dinners!'

The Marshal fished two thousand-lire notes out of his top pocket. The lads could share them with him after lunch.

He left the piazza at the end near the church, and crossed Via Maggio. The road was already empty and the shops closed; it must be after one. He glanced at his watch: ten past. Then he remembered Signora Giusti, and paused. He could smell the peaches, cool and heavy in their brown bag. He was thirsty, tired and hot, and his meal, collected from the mensa by Lorenzini, would be spoiling. The street was silent except for occasional muffled sounds of crockery and women's voices. A narrow strip of blue sky ran overhead between the dark eaves. He thought of the tiny old lady in her flat, sitting alone, waiting . . . and he turned back.

She lived on the top floor in the corner by the church. There was a goldsmith's workshop in the ground floor left, and on the right was a tiny place, hardly more than a hole in the wall, that sold flowers. Both had their metal shutters down. He rang the top bell and stepped back on to litter-strewn cobbles, expecting a face to appear at the window since there was no housephone. But the door opened immediately; she must have been waiting beside the switch. Inside, on the left, was a door with a frosted glass panel in it and a brass plate beside it saying 'Giuseppe Pratesi, Goldsmith and Jeweller.' The flower-seller's tiny den was entered directly from the piazza. Nevertheless, the scent of flowers mingled with the smell of metal filings and gas burners as the Marshal began to climb slowly up the gloomy staircase, having looked in vain for a lift. A thin rope, worn smooth by many hands, served as a banister; it was looped through black iron protruberances set into the pitted walls at each turn in the staircase. Each floor had two brown-varnished doors with big brass doorknobs.

She was waiting for him inside her doorway, and she began to cry as soon as he came into view, hat in hand, on the last flight. He was too out of breath to speak and made no effort to interrupt her first tirade as he followed her inside.

'And it's hours since I telephoned, but nobody listens to an old woman—I could be robbed of what few scraps I have left in this world—but that witch won't get me out! They don't know what it's like to be old and defence-less . . .'

He almost had to run to keep up with her because the straight-backed chair on castors, which was supposed to help her to walk, careered madly along the tiled corridor with her tiny figure tottering after it, chattering and wailing as it went. The flat was long and narrow, all the main rooms opening off the left side of the passage. The bedroom door was always open to reveal the scanty furniture inside it, but all the other big rooms, the Marshal knew from Lorenzini, were bare. Over the years she'd had to sell her good old furniture bit by bit. They came to rest in the kitchen at the end of the passage.

'Sit down.' The old lady had already settled her frail bones into a battered leather armchair filled with an assortment of crocheted and flower-printed cushions by the window. Before her was a low table with the telephone on a crocheted mat, a list of numbers written in large red print and a magnifying glass. She indicated the hard chair opposite her as the place where he should sit.

'And what are the sunglasses in aid of?'

'Excuse me.' He took them off and slid them into his top pocket. 'It's an allergy I have . . . the sun upsets my eyes . . .'

'Not in here it won't!'

It was true that the room was gloomy; the window overlooked a narrow, sunless courtyard. She must spend the day keeping an eye on the doings of her neighbours, sometimes trundling herself and her wheeled chair through to the bedroom to watch the busy piazza. Those eight flights of stone stairs . . . it must have been years since she last left the building.

The old lady was quick to catch his sympathetic glance and play on it.

'You see what it comes to in the end? Stuck here alone day after day and not a soul ever to come near me. I haven't been out of this house for over sixteen years . . . just sitting here all alone . . . day after day . . .'

Big tears were beginning to spurt from her eyes and she took a handkerchief from her dress pocket.

'But the woman from the Council comes, surely, Signora? Doesn't she do your shopping, wash and dress you, prepare your meal?'

'That witch! I'm talking about friends, friends who should visit me, not servants! Do you think I'd have allowed a woman like that into my home when my husband was alive? But it doesn't do to have standards these days. Tinned food, she once tried to bring into this house, but I drew the line there all right. I told her straight . . .'

She had done better than that, as the Marshal recalled; she had thrown the little tin of jellied chicken at the unfortunate young woman's head, cutting it badly. Lorenzini had arrived in the middle of the row, having been called out to investigate Signora Giusti's complaint about the youngsters on the floor below having their stereo on at full volume, and he had found the social worker sobbing and holding a wet towel to her temple which was bleeding profusely. Lorenzini had brought the young students up with him to try and make peace, and a couple from the second floor had arrived on the scene to find out what the din was about; the husband was a street cleaner who worked nights and had been trying to get some sleep. There had hardly been room for all these people in the small kitchen, and Signora Giusti, Lorenzini reported, had been in her element, alternately weeping and chattering, content to be getting the amount of attention she considered her due.

Even so, the Marshal thought, as the tiny, bird-like creature twittered on about the evil doings of the Council social worker, there was no getting away from the fact that she *was* ninety-one, and that she could hardly hope to leave her flat again except when she left it in her coffin.

'. . . Telling me I should be grateful! Grateful! That the only person I see all day is a stranger who thinks she has the run of the house, who tells me what to do and what to eat . . . she even cut my hair off, do you know that? My beautiful hair . . .'

She was crying in earnest now, apparently, although you could never be sure. Certainly, her hair which was fine and white and fairly plentiful, considering her age, had been cut off just below her ears like a little girl's.

'Maybe she thought you'd find it easier,' murmured the Marshal unhappily. He remembered that they'd cut his mother's hair after the stroke three months ago . . . but she really was like a child now, and it hadn't been a stranger who'd done it, but his wife. Was it possible to be still vain at ninety-one?

On the shiny yellow kitchen wall, next to a gaudy coloured print of Pope John XXIII surrounded by a border of old Christmas tinsel and topped by a red plastic rose, there was a group of framed family photographs; good frames, too, probably silver. One of them was of an exceptionally beautiful girl with abundant dark hair, a high lace collar and heavy strings of pearls. The Marshal had been admiring it absent-mindedly for some minutes before he realized with a start that it must be Signora Giusti herself. She must have been used to a lot of attention all right, and now . . . There were patches on the wall where two other photographs had been. Had she been obliged to sell the silver frames?

'She won't get me out! I won't be turned out of my own home as if I were a nobody, leaving the place to be ransacked. I've told her I could be robbed, but all she cares about is going off on holiday—that's the sort of person I have to let into my home! That's the sort of treatment I'm supposed to be grateful for— but I'll not go and she can't make me! You'll have to tell her. Coming from you . . .'

But the Marshal had completely lost track.

'I'm not sure I understand. Who wants you to go where?'

Her incessant chatter was exhausting him. He was hungry and tired, but she was as lively as ever, the frail little body rattling about in the big armchair, back erect, eyes and hands constantly in motion.

'I've already explained once, if you'd been listening, that she's trying to get rid of me for a month, put me in a hospital while she goes off on holiday — like putting a dog in kennels — '

'I see . . . you mean the social worker. But this hospital — '

'Well, it's not a hospital, not exactly, more of a convalescent home. Out in the hills. Supposed to be cooler than Florence.'

'I imagine it must be if it's out in the hills — and you know, Signora, this young woman, the social worker . . . what is she called?'

'I wouldn't know,' snapped Signora Giusti untruthfully.

'Well, I expect she has a family, has to take her holiday when the children are off school.'

'Then they should send me someone else, not shunt me about like a useless bundle of rags!'

She was weeping again.

The Marshal sighed. He couldn't imagine why she wanted to drag him into all this, but he felt sorry for the social worker who must be suffering this sort of thing every morning. He tried a different approach.

'Listen, Signora — ' he leaned forward heavily — 'you must remember that in a sense you're a very exceptional person . . .'

She stopped crying and began to pay attention.

'There are other people of your age in Florence, but I doubt if any of them have kept themselves in trim the way you have, kept their interest in life, kept their wits about them — you know what I mean.'

'Hm,' said the Signora, sniffing. 'Florentines.'

'There's never enough staff during the summer . . .' He was treading carefully. 'And nor are there many places in the . . . convalescent homes out in the country. It's a question of choosing who to offer them to, choosing people who are capable of taking advantage of it . . .'

'Very good. Very nicely put. And who chooses where *you* go for your holidays?'

'I . . .'

'And I'll choose where to go for mine! And it won't be a place like that, I can promise you.'

'But how do you know, until you've been, what—'

'I have been.'

'You have? When?'

'I forget. But I won't set foot in a place run by a woman like that.'

'What woman?'

'The matron.' She leaned towards him and explained confidentially, 'A southerner. You understand me. They're not like us.'

'We're all Italians,' murmured the Marshal, staring. He came from Sicily.

'*We* are. But not southerners. Some of them are practically Negroes. Or else Arabs. They won't work and they live like animals. Where are you going?'

The Marshal had risen.

'If you're wondering where to put that—I hope it's fruit; it's the only thing I can enjoy with no teeth, that and cake—but you'd be surprised how many people come round here empty-handed. Or else they bring me hard stuff I can't possibly eat. That looks like fruit.'

'Peaches.' The Marshal resigned himself. It was true that he hadn't thought of bringing her anything, that he'd almost forgotten to come at all.

'Put them in the fridge. You've brought too many, they'll go off before I can eat them. Over there, behind that bit of curtain.'

She really was impossible!

He opened the rickety fridge which could have done with cleaning. There was a saucer on the middle shelf with a ball of cooked spinach on it. A small box of sterilized milk in the door. Nothing else. He put the peaches in the plastic bin at the bottom.

'Not there.' She was behind him, leaning on the wheeled chair. 'I can't bend down.'

He moved the peaches higher up. Next to the fridge was an old gas cooker with a battered saucepan on it containing the remains of the milky coffee which the social worker prepared in the mornings.

'*She* makes it,' commented Signora Giusti, 'and I heat it up after I've eaten my meal. But today I dropped the matches. I couldn't fancy drinking it cold. I suppose you wouldn't . . .'

The matches were down between the fridge and the cooker. The Marshal picked them up and lit the gas. She watched him quietly, worried, perhaps, that she had gone too far since he didn't speak.

'Not too hot . . .'

She sat in her chair and he gave her the plastic beaker of warm coffee. She was a pathetic figure once she stopped being bloody-minded.

'Now, Signora, I'll have to go.'

'Wait . . .' She pulled herself to her feet and reached for her walking chair. 'There's something I've got to show you.'

She tottered off, rattling down the passage to her bedroom, the Marshal following resignedly.

There was nothing in the huge shuttered room except one of what had obviously been a pair of high wooden beds, and a cheap plywood chest of drawers. The bed had a dusty wooden cherub sitting on top of the headboard, raising a plump finger to its lips for quiet. The other bed with its cherub, the wardrobe and the dressing-table had

evidently been sold. So, very probably, had the carpets;
there was a bit of cheap matting by the bed.

Signora Giusti was fishing, with some difficulty, under
the mattress.

'Help me . . .'

He heaved the mattress up and her tiny hand grasped a
leather pouch. She put it under his nose and said:

'There! A hundred thousand lire. Don't tell a soul.' She
pushed it back out of sight.

'That's my burial money. I know I can trust you.
You're a family man. It's the one thing, now, that matters
to me . . . to be buried respectably. You know what I
mean . . .'

He knew what she meant. To be 'buried respectably'
meant to be buried in an airtight compartment, or
loculo, set into specially constructed walls, with a
memorial plaque and an icon light in front. These apartments for the dead, with their rows of red lights winking
in the darkness, varied in price according to their position
in the wall, but they were always expensive. For those who
couldn't afford them, burial in the ground was free, but
not permanent. After ten years the body had to be
exhumed, identified, and the remains put into a small
ossuary and sealed at last into a smaller, permanent
loculo. If there was still no money to pay for it, or if
nobody turned up to identify the body and foot the bill,
the remains were disposed of at the discretion of the sani-
tary department.

'You understand—' Signora Giusti clutched urgently at
his arm—'I have nobody . . . If they don't bury me
respectably what will happen to my poor old bones?'

She was weeping again.

'Now that you know where the money is . . . you'll see to
it . . . you'll tell them . . .'

'I'll tell them.'

'I'm not a pauper yet . . . Oh, if you'd seen how beautiful I was as a girl you'd understand! I don't want to end up on some rubbish heap . . . you must see that they take the photograph that's on the wall in the kitchen, don't forget that.'

It was customary to reproduce a photograph on a little ceramic plaque to be placed by the icon light.

'I won't forget.'

'You're a respectable person so I can trust you. I daren't tell anyone else, you see, because of the money. I don't want to be robbed.'

'I'll see to it. Don't worry.'

How could he tell her she was years behind the times, that to be 'buried respectably' these days would cost her between a million and two million lire? Her precious little bag of money would only pay for flowers and the photograph.

There was nothing he could say.

'I'll have to be going . . .'

'But you will speak to that woman from the Council? You'll explain why I have to stay here and defend my last few lire?'

'But I don't come into it. There's no reason why she should bother about what I say . . .'

'She'll have to listen to you, don't you understand? Because of the prowler in the flat next door.'

'*The prowler?*'

'Yes, the prowler! Well, that's what I called you for! I explained it all to that boy who answered the phone — surely he told you?'

'Of course he did, yes . . .' He'd never thought to ask what . . . 'The flat next door. It's been empty for years, hasn't it? And you think there's been somebody in there?'

'I know there has. There's nothing wrong with my hearing.'

'Don't you think it could have been the owner?'

'Can't have been. When he comes back the first thing

he does is to come and see me. I practically brought him up. I looked after him when his mother died, poor woman — of course her husband was a foreigner, you know, so . . . Anyway, the child spent as much time in this house as he did in his own, and I was the one who nursed him when he had rheumatic fever — called me his *mammina*, he did — at least until his father married again — so don't try and tell me it was him, or her either, for that matter — the stepmother, I mean, because apart from her being a foreigner, not Dutch, he was Dutch but she was English, I won't hear a word said against her. It was a sad day for me when she packed up and left. I never needed any social worker when I had her for a neighbour. If she came back, and I wish to God that she would, she wouldn't be sneaking around in the middle of the night, she'd come straight here to see me!'

The Marshal wearily followed the tottering little figure back along the passage to the kitchen, and there he took out a handkerchief, mopped his brow and sat down again on the hard chair.

Glancing at the list of numbers written large by the telephone, he saw the general emergency number, 113, listed between himself and the grocer. He wondered if she ever called the Police instead of the Carabinieri. Perhaps she took them in turn . . .

He brought out his notebook and a ballpoint pen.

'You heard a prowler in the night. When?'

'Last night, of course! I would hardly wait a week to call you!'

'Last night. What time?'

'First at just after seven-thirty.'

'That's not the middle of the night.'

'Wait. Somebody went in there just after seven-thirty. I heard the door shut. I was in bed. I'm always in bed by seven-thirty because there's nothing much to do — I don't have a television because it would hurt my eyes, besides which I can't afford it. So, I go to bed, despite the dreadful noise in the piazza that shouldn't be allowed. Anyway, a bit later than that—I was still listening because, to tell you the truth, I was still hoping it might be him or his stepmother and that there might be a knock at my door, and then I heard someone else go in . . .'

'Are you sure it wasn't the same person going out?'

She gave him a withering look.

'The second person went in, and not long after that there was a row.'

'A noise, you mean?'

'No, a row. A quarrel. A quite violent quarrel, things knocked over, if not thrown. Then one of them left. The woman who went in last.'

'How do you know it was a woman?'

Another withering look.

'High heels. Stone stairs. My bedroom's right by the front door, as you've seen.'

'And the other one?'

'A man. I heard his voice raised during the quarrel. And he's still in there. I didn't sleep all night, I just listened. I heard him crashing about, quite late on, as if he were in a temper.'

'You didn't get up? Peep out?'

'I can't. I can get myself into bed with a little stool and my chair to help me, but I can't get out. It's too high, and I've fallen I don't know how many times. Can you imagine what it's like to lie on the floor all night? One of these days they'll find me dead . . . I have to wait for *her* to come. She has a key. All morning I've been behind the front door—I didn't tell *her* anything, just rang you as soon as she'd gone—and I had to ring twice before anybody took any notice, remember that! Now then. What if it's squatters . . . young people these days . . . that house is still furnished, do you know that? And if they can get in there they can get in here, and I won't have it! I'm not leaving here for a month and letting any Tom, Dick and Harry lay his hands on the few scraps and sticks I have left in this world . . . and my burial money . . .'

She fished out the little handkerchief.

'Calm down now, Signora, calm down. You don't seem to have thought of the one simple solution—that the house might have been let?'

'Without anyone knowing? And anyway, he uses it. Only a couple of times a year, as a rule, but he never fails to visit me. And if he'd decided to let it he'd have said, knowing how particular I am about the sort of neighbours . . .'

'All right, all right. In that case, since you say there's somebody still in there, I'll go across and see.'

She followed him to the front door, rattling along with her chair.

The door across the hall still had a printed nameplate saying T. Goossens.

'You see,' said Signora Giusti behind him. 'Dutch. His first wife was Italian. He's dead now, of course. It's the son who still comes. Ton, they christened him, but I always called him Toni.'

The Marshal rang the bell.

They waited some time but no one answered.

'Would a squatter answer?' whispered Signora Giusti at his elbow.

'I'm not sure,' said the Marshal. 'Possibly not if he'd seen me arrive. But I don't think, myself, that there's a squatter here.'

He rang again and then looked through the keyhole, but it was impossible to see anything. Perhaps the hallway was as dark as Signora Giusti's.

'The other one,' she said impatiently. 'The old keyhole, lower down. You should be able to see the entire house through it.'

The old keyhole was a good three inches high. He

crouched and peered through. He sat back on his heels, blinked, and peered again. The hall, like Signora Giusti's, was long, narrow and gloomy. The doors in this flat opened on the right.

'Can you see anything?'

'Nothing.' He straightened up. 'Can I use your telephone?'

'So, you believe me now?'

'I believe you.'

'Even though you can't see anything?'

'As a matter of fact, I heard something. Is it likely that the owner would go off leaving the tap running?'

'Good heavens no! He turned the water off at the mains. Everything else, too.'

'Hm. There's a tap running in there. I'll have to use your telephone. I can't go in there without a warrant.'

'No, but I can. I wasn't going in there on my own.'

She wheeled herself round and reached for a bunch of keys that was hanging on a hook behind her front door.

'He left me a set. You see how it is? He was like a son to me. Once or twice when he's been back—always on business; he's a jeweller—he's brought his wife with him. She likes to buy clothes here; they're well off, you see. In that case he used to telephone me and I'd go in and open the windows, air the place a bit. I can't do more these days. Usually, though, he turns up by himself and so doesn't bother. If he trusts me with the keys it's so I can keep an eye on things, and I'm not going in there without you.'

She handed him the keys, and after a moment's hesitation, the Marshal unlocked the door without touching it.

'Wait there. Better still, go back behind your own door.'

He was certain she would come creeping out again as soon as his back was turned.

He went towards the sound of running water, drawing out his Beretta as he went. But there was no feeling of life

in the flat, only of something being wrong. In the bathroom, water was running into the sink which was filled to
overflowing, evidently partially blocked by vomit, some of
which was floating on the water's surface. The contents of
the bathroom cabinet had been tumbled out on to the
floor, and there were pieces of broken glass and streaks of
blood in the bath and on the grey floor tiles. The Marshal
looked about for a towel and, not finding one, took out
his handkerchief and turned off the tap with one finger.

The door to the kitchen at the end of the corridor was
open, and he could see, even at a distance, that there was
a mess in there, too. Going along the marble-tiled
passage, he could smell fresh coffee. Probably it had been
spilled.

There was a tiny sound. The Marshal stopped and
whipped round. It could just be Signora Giusti following
him . . . but she made more noise than that, and she was
nowhere in sight. He began to walk back along the corridor, quickly, almost running. He went to the bedroom
by instinct. The room nearest the door, like Signora
Giusti's. With the handkerchief still in his hand he tried
to open the door, but it wouldn't move. How did he
know, as sure as if he could see through the door, what
sort of thing he would find? Nothing quite like it had ever
happened to him before. He turned the handle and pushed
steadily but gently until he heard the man's body fall over
with a soft thud. As if drawn by the same knowledge,
Signora Giusti came rattling along the passage.

'What is it? What have you found? Is someone dead?'

The Marshal turned from what he had been contem-
plating and withdrew from the room to turn her away.

'Do you have the number of the *Misericordia* on your
telephone list?'

'Of course I have, but what's happened?'

'Go and call them, will you?'

Quieted by his manner, the old lady rattled away

towards her own flat, then stopped and called out:

'But I ought to tell them — is he dead?'

The Marshal switched on the weak centre light in the bedroom, then one of the bedside lamps.

'I think so . . .'

Why had he said that, when before he had been sure . . . ?

The man, though young, was very heavily built, and the Marshal doubted whether he could lift him on to the high wooden bed. He got a pillow which had no slip on it and some of its musty feathers poking through the greyish cloth, turned the body over, and propped up the head. A bunch of keys fell to the floor. There was no sign of life, and the face was ashen, the lips blue. And yet . . . The Marshal bent and put an ear to the chest. Nothing. Maybe the pulse . . .

The man's hands had been slashed and impaled by pieces of glass. They were big hands, but the fingertips were highly articulate, almost delicate. Wrapped around one hand was the towel that the Marshal had sought in the bathroom. So, he had tried to bind up his cuts, perhaps, or at least stop them bleeding. There seemed to be no pulse and yet, still the Marshal was not convinced. Something was bothering him — the little noise he had heard? Could have been a mouse, something falling over, the body settling. But his hands . . .

Suddenly he got to his feet and strode out into the passage. Signora Giusti was trundling back in at the front door.

'Go back!' he called, 'and let me use your phone.'

'They're already on their way . . .'

'It doesn't matter . . . I should have thought . . .'

He dialled the *Misericordia* number and spoke hurriedly with the Servant.

'I should have thought of it before, but there are so many other things wrong with him . . . It was only when I realized that one of the cuts was still bleeding just a little . . .'

'The coronary unit will be with you in less than five minutes.'

The doorbell was ringing urgently. The first ambulance had already arrived.

'I gave them my name,' said Signora Giusti, tottering rapidly to the front door. 'No use their ringing there if . . .'

The Marshal was back beside the body when the four Brothers of the *Misericordia* came in. One of them was very young, not much more than sixteen, and wore his black gown and hood self-consciously. He didn't look at the body but at the senior Brother, waiting for instructions.

'Can we put him on the bed a moment?' asked the Marshal.

'We'll see to it.'

The four Brothers lifted the big man expertly and laid him on the bed. The senior Brother looked at the Marshal, who said:

"I just wasn't sure. There's something . . . I called back for the coronary unit.'

'I'd say you did right. That's them now.'

The siren was wailing outside, breaking into the peace of siesta-time.

'I'll go and meet them—frankly, I'd say it would be fatal to move him at all, but they might be able to do something on the spot . . .'

The other three were taking off the man's tie and unbuttoning his shirt. He was wearing one slipper. The young boy took it off carefully, then stood back. The Marshal kept an eye on him.

'Is it your first time out?'

'Yes.' He was very pale, but calm. Occasionally he fingered the huge black rosary which the Brothers wore as a belt.

'Toni! It's my Toni!'

'Signora!' The Marshal cursed himself for having forgotten her. 'Come away; they'll do all they can.'

'No! I'm staying. I'll keep out of the way but I'm staying. If they bring him to he'll recognize me; he'll tell me what's happened.'

She wheeled herself over to one of the windows and tried to open the shutters with one hand.

'Help me.'

The doctor and his assistant had come into the room without a word and were making a rapid examination of the man on the bed. The doctor prepared to do a massage whilst his assistant plugged in a portable monitor.

The Marshal wrenched open the inner shutters, the window, then the brown louvred shutters on the outside. The sunlight blinded him. He had almost forgotten it was still daytime. A small crowd had gathered on the pavement. He closed the window and switched off the electric lights which were practically invisible in the beam of sunlight coming in at the window. Only then did he notice that the bed hadn't been made up. There was just a cotton counterpane covering the bare mattress which was visible near the pillow.

The doctor had paused and now he lifted the patient's eyelids.

'I'm afraid it's far too late,' he said quietly. 'It was you who found him?'

'Yes . . .'

'There's some response but it won't last. Apart from the heart attack I'd say he'd probably taken a massive dose of sleeping pills, and to try and pump his stomach now would kill him. Is the old lady his mother?'

'A neighbour who's known him since he was a child. Actually, she's old enough to be his grandmother. Is there any chance he'll come round before . . . ?'

'Not much. Why? Do you think there's foul play involved?'

'Don't you?'

'I wouldn't like to say without further information.

However, I can inject a stimulant and we'll see . . .

'It won't harm him?'

'It's either that or letting him sink into a coma.'

Signora Giusti pushed herself towards the bed, and the Marshal brought a chair up for her, wheeling her own out of the way.

'Toni! What's happened to you? Tell me what's happened?'

She wanted to touch him but his hands were covered in dried blood, the hair wet and streaked with vomit. She took her tiny handkerchief and wiped his face with small dabbing movements as she must have done when he was a small boy with rheumatic fever.

'Toni . . .'

His colour, especially about the lips, was slightly better.

The old lady's shaky, age-spotted hands went on dabbing and stroking as though she could soothe away whatever was happening to him.

'Toni, it's me.'

It was as if the man's eyes opened by her willpower rather than his own volition. He was evidently unable to focus on any of the faces surrounding him.

'It's me, Toni, your old *mammina*.'

The man's lips and fingers twitched slightly. He might have been trying to speak or it might have been the effect of the drug. His lips were parched and one of the Brothers came forward with a little water and wet them.

The doctor, who was preparing to leave, looked at the Marshal and shook his head.

The senior Brother had slipped away quietly, and he came back now with the priest from Santo Spirito. The Marshal touched Signora Giusti gently.

'The priest is here. But if his father was Dutch, perhaps . . .'

'No, no, he was brought up a Catholic. His mother . . . I dressed him myself for his First Communion.'

The priest unrolled his stole and put it on carefully. He beckoned the youngest brother, saying in a stage whisper:

'You know how to help me?'

The boy nodded and took his place beside the priest who whispered again, this time to the senior Brother:

'If you would find me a bit of linen, anything at all, so long as it's clean . . . and a little water . . .'

He was an old man and not at all perturbed by unusual circumstances, or by occasionally having to welcome or dispatch his parishioners in a hurry with the aid of a hastily rinsed jam-jar and a tea-towel.

A small jug of water was produced, a scrap of bread from Signora Giusti's kitchen, and a white damask cloth from the marble-topped chest of drawers in the bedroom. The priest spread the cloth on a small bedside table, laid out his silver containers and lit a candle.

The dusty shaft of sunlight from the one unshuttered window lit the bed and its half-naked occupant, and the small bent figure of the old lady beside it. The priest in his white surplice and purple stole murmured a *confiteor* and then moved forward into the sunbeam and lifted his pale hand to grant the Dutchman a plenary indulgence and the remission of all his sins.

'In the name of the Father and of the Son and of the Holy Ghost.'

'Amen.'

The three Brothers knelt down in the gloom at the foot of the bed with a faint rustle of their black cotton gowns and a click as their dangling rosary belts touched the marble floor. The Marshal's pale bulk was just visible, very still, in the far corner of the room.

The priest turned and whispered to the boy who handed him the tiny silver container of oil. He dipped his thumb into it and made a cross on each of the Dutchman's eyelids.

'Through this holy oil and through His everlasting

mercy, may Our Lord Jesus Christ forgive you all the sins you have committed with your sight.'

'Amen.'

The boy wiped away the oil with cotton-wool while the priest anointed the nostrils.

'Through this holy oil and through His everlasting mercy . . .'

A little whimper escaped the old lady's lips, but she was probably unconscious of it, her eyes fixed on the Dutchman's face, not following the movements of the pale, dry hand that gently touched the parched lips and the ears in turn and then reached over towards the wrist she was holding.

'. . . Forgive you all the sins you have committed by your touch . . .'

The cross of oil glistened in the palm of the bloodied hand. The boy dabbed it away and, at a glance from the priest, moved down the bed to uncover the feet, rolling back grey silk socks.

'Through this holy oil . . .'

The old lady's eyes never left the dying man's face. Perhaps she was seeing not the man but the little boy she had nursed through his fever long ago.

The half-lit room was musty and airless, and the Marshal, who had not eaten or drunk for many hours, felt his mouth uncomfortably dry. He ought to be formulating a report in his mind, but the stillness of the room and the priest's rhythmic movements and droning voice were hypnotic. The noise of children and dogs running round in the piazza below came from another world where people were waking from their siesta and going about their business.

'For the sins you have committed . . .'

'Amen.'

The priest wiped his thumb on the small piece of bread and held his hands over a silver bowl to let the boy pour a trickle of water over them.

'Our Father . . .' He continued the prayer silently, and the only movement was of dust revolving in the shaft of sunlight, until he raised his head and continued aloud: 'And lead us not into temptation.'

'But deliver us from evil.'

Another rustle and a faint chink as the Brothers got to their feet. It was over. The priest and the boy were quietly packing everything they had used, including the scrap of bread and the stained cotton-wool which had to be taken back to the church and burnt. There was no sound or sign from the Dutchman who must surely die any minute. The Marshal slipped out of the bedroom, hoping to find a telephone in one of the other rooms. It was obvious that this wasn't going to be a job an NCO could deal with and he would have to telephone Headquarters who would send an officer to take charge. He found a phone in the sitting room where the white shapes of dust-sheeted furniture were visible in the shuttered gloom. The line was dead and he had to creep back into the bedroom to get the keys to Signora Giusti's flat.

'Hello? Guarnaccia, stazione Pitti . . . yes, again . . .'

But that first call, from the Pensione Giulia, seemed to have happened in another age, so strongly did the dying man dominate everyone and everything in his immediate surroundings.

'And you'll inform the Public Prosecutor? Yes . . . no, there's no need; the *Misericordia* will take him straight to the Medico-Legal Institute. And there's no great hurry. . .' He didn't want the whole bustling crew turning up before the poor man was even dead. Although perhaps by now . . .

But the Dutchman was still alive. The priest had left and the senior Brother was sitting beside the bed holding one of the dying man's arms while Signora Giusti held the other. The Marshal came and stood beside her, wondering whether, at her age, she could take all this upset.

'Signora . . .'

'I'm all right. Leave me here with him.'

Perhaps this time he recognized her voice. He couldn't have seen her for his eyes remained closed, but he spoke suddenly in a firm, almost normal voice:

'*Mammina?*'

'I'm here. I'm right beside you. You're going to be all right.'

'It wasn't her.' There was silence for a while. Then he said wearily, 'Pain . . .' Shortly after that, one eye opened slightly and stayed open while his last faint breath rattled weakly in his throat and stopped.

CHAPTER 2

'What about his suitcase?'

'Take it with you as it is. And this, and these keys . . .'

'Oh! Luciani! Take care of these!'

'Try and open that shutter. The light in here . . .'

'Make way, will you? The doctor's arrived . . .'

The flat was crowded with people, some of whom were carrying things away, and others who were examining things on the spot, all of them raising clouds of dust everywhere they went. The photographer's flashes lit the bedroom intermittently. When the doctor came up he had to step over the scratched, black metal coffin that was blocking the narrow passage. It wasn't Professor Forli, but a younger man who had just become his assistant. He was very reserved and formal and didn't chat to anyone as Forli would have done while preparing to make his examination.

The Marshal had said his piece, taken Signora Giusti back to her flat and returned, as unobtrusively as he could, to watch the technicians at work. It was a business he disliked, this dismantling of a person's life to examine it under a microscope, and he could not have said himself why he was still there. He knew he was in the way as he pushed along the corridor to the kitchen to watch a white-coated man systematically collecting the remains of a meal and an almost empty pot of coffee. There were coffee grains all over the floor and a lot of dried blood under the table.

The latest person to arrive was the Substitute Prosecutor, the jacket of his white linen suit swinging open, his striped shirt a little tight about the paunch. He was out of breath and pink in the face from hurrying up eight flights of stairs, and not a little irritated at having been disturbed after a heavy luncheon-party and made to rush about in the heat looking for his registrar.

'Well? Tell me?'

He hardly looked at the officer in charge as he spoke. The Marshal came back to the bedroom doorway and watched. He didn't know the officer, who was very young and a little nervous. Could it be his first case? At any rate, after making his report he continued to give his men orders but glanced worriedly at the Substitute Prosecutor each time, as if expecting approval or correction.

'In other words, a suicide,' said the Substitute Prosecutor, after listening with unconcealed impatience to the young doctor's solemn and meticulous preliminary report, 'albeit a messy one. Changed his mind half way, d'you think?'

'It's possible. But there are one or two things . . .'

'Well, the autopsy should clear them up.' He turned back to the officer: 'Who is he? Do we know?'

'A Dutchman—or rather, Italo-Dutch. He was born here in Florence of a Dutch father and an Italian mother, both deceased, but there is a surviving stepmother, present whereabouts unknown but thought likely to be in England, according to the next-door neighbour here who

knew her well. He has a wife and a mother-in-law in
Amsterdam. We're going through his papers now for the
address.'

'Hm. Good.'

The young officer glanced gratefully at the Marshal
who remained silent and impassive in the doorway, his
eyes occasionally scanning the room.

The Substitute Prosecutor was anxious to leave, but the
Examining Magistrate still hadn't turned up. Waiting, he
said:

'A Dutchman. There won't be any diplomatic repercus-
sion? He wasn't . . . ?'

'No,' the officer said, 'I don't think so. He was a
jeweller and goldsmith, quite well-to-do, nothing more.'

'Good. Well, let his wife know as soon as possible. Best
do it through the Dutch Consulate, Via Cavour . . .'

It was a struggle to get the metal coffin down the staircase, and all four Brothers were perspiring under their
black hoods by the time they reached street level. The
crowd stood back and watched it loaded into the *Misericordia* van, and the Marshal, who had followed it down,
heard them murmuring:

'Poor old creature . . .'

'She was over ninety, of course . . .'

'Even so, they say it was suicide . . . or worse, and the
place is full of police . . .'

The shops around the piazza were rolling up their
metal shutters, the noisy signal that they were about to
open for the evening. But the heat, at five o'clock, was
just as intense as ever, and the suffocating blast that had
hit the Marshal as he came out of the dark doorway
dismayed him. He had never got used to the humid heat
of Florence, so unlike the dry, burning days down south,
even though he had been there six years, not counting his
days in the non-commissioned officers' school.

The heat never seemed to come from the sun but to rise

in oppressive waves from the heated stones of the buildings, imprisoning the city in a hot cloud that got progressively sweatier and more exhaust-laden as the day went on. The feeling of asphyxiation was so intense that the Marshal often felt the urge to open a window in order to breathe, and then he would remember that he was outside.

On the opposite side of the piazza stood the cool-looking bar, large and tiled, that sold drinks and home-made ice-cream, but when the Marshal reached it he saw that the cash desk was thronged with half-dressed young tourists queuing for receipts before choosing their ice-cream. The only alternative to queuing would be to sit at one of the white tables under the trees and be waited on, but he couldn't see himself doing that. It would cost double, anyway.

He made his way out of the piazza and eventually found a bar with no queue, a small, dark place with a pinball machine in the back and hundreds of assorted, dusty bottles on the shelves. The proprietor, whose grey hair was cut *en brosse*, wore a faded maroon jacket and a bow tie, as if he had once worked in a big restaurant.

'A coffee and a glass of water.' He took a couple of brioches from the clear plastic box on the bar.

'Hot,' remarked the barman, by way of conversation. 'We should be at the seaside, not working. But I don't go anymore, what with the crowds and the expense. It said on the news last night that, apart from your pensione or whatever, you need between eighty and a hundred thousand lire a day at the seaside.'

'I can believe it.'

'Five thousand a day just to go on the beach, deck-chair and umbrella and whatnot, ice-cream for the kids twice what it cost last year—mine are grown up, thank God, and they take their kids camping.'

'Good idea,' said the Marshal, munching.

'That's what I say. Even so, things are not what they were.'

'They're not. How much do I owe you?'

'One thousand exactly—there are some charging twice that price across the river but it's madness, that's what I say. Where's it all going to end if we're all greedy . . .'

The Station was very quiet when he got back to Pitti. The downstairs office was empty, and the only sounds were the whining of the fan and a spasmodic tapping noise, interspersed with long, thoughtful pauses. There was no need to ask who it was.

'Aoh! Ciccio!'

The Marshal was smiling, as everyone did, just at the thought of the roly-poly fair-haired boy. He soon appeared, lolloping slowly down the stairs, his shirt collar open and his tie askew.

'You're all alone?'

'Yes, sir. Lorenzini and di Nuccio went out in the van to collect the post.'

'Any calls?'

'No, sir.'

It was always the same; if there was a desirable errand to do such as collecting the post which came up by courier from General Command in Rome, or even going round to the mensa to collect the lunches, Gino would let the other two go. But when it came to going for bread or water to the grocer down in the piazza there would be the usual argument about whose turn it was, followed by Gino's saying cheerfully, 'I'll go.'

The Marshal looked at his watch.

'Have they been gone long?'

'Not very long.' Gino blushed, knowing as well as the Marshal knew that they would find five minutes for a quick coffee and a chat with old friends and acquaintances.

'And what about you going for the post now and then?

Don't you like to have a chat to the other lads occasionally, eh?'

'I've got my brother, Marshal.' Gino smiled, pink with pleasure.

It was true that they never lost an opportunity to be together. Sometimes they went to the cinema, sometimes they just walked round town. Sergio, the elder brother, had been admitted to the non-commissioned officers' school. Gino, as a consequence, worshipped him more than ever, if that were possible. But nothing the Marshal could say would persuade him to apply for admission to the school himself.

'My brother has all the brains,' he would say. 'He's always been brighter than me.'

'But you've got to think of the future. It's no joke having to retire at an age when you've still got young children to bring up.'

'But nobody would marry me, Marshal. Sergio's always been the good-looking one of the family.' And he would blush more furiously than ever.

The Marshal brooded over all his lads, but he had a real soft spot for Gino who reminded him rather of himself at the same age. He too had been a peasant's son, overweight and awkward. But not, he reflected now, quite so naif; it took a northern country bumpkin for that. Gino had never seen a foreigner before he joined up. Well, he was still very young, there was plenty of time for him to change his mind.

'I'm going to have a rest for half an hour.' He patted the boy on the shoulder and opened the door that led to his quarters. 'No doubt the others will be back by then. I'll have to go out again afterwards and finish my hotel round . . .'

In the cool, dark living-room where the shutters had been closed all day, the Marshal took off his jacket and shirt, sat down in his armchair, and heaved his feet on to a stool. He had thought he wanted to sleep but he found himself wakeful. It was only peace he needed, to let certain images roll through his mind. Some of them returned repeatedly: the humped figure behind the door, a nervous, black-hooded boy carefully rolling back a grey silk sock, lumps of vomit swirling round in the water under a running tap . . . and that tiny noise that had sent him running to the bedroom. Had the man been conscious? Had that tiny noise cost him enormous effort? Other images appeared, too: of the man blundering around the flat . . . 'Crashing about as if he were in a temper.' More like a wounded animal . . . And he had cut his hands, somehow, and then tried to bind them up clumsily with a towel. Suicide . . . why should the Substitute Prosecutor think that? Surely it was obvious . . . But perhaps he didn't know yet about the woman. Had he told the officer in charge about Signora Giusti's having heard a woman? If he hadn't . . . what a terrible mistake . . . how could he have forgotten a thing so important . . . the woman . . . He could see her malicious little eyes, her tight lips, that smirk of selfish satisfaction as the priest raised his hand to give absolution . . . Yet surely, she hadn't been there then? The Dutchman had said it wasn't her . . .

The Marshal realized, seconds before it happened, that he was falling asleep after all.

Di Nuccio's voice woke him with the suddenness of a gunshot, although he had only spoken quietly out in the office. The Marshal's mouth was dry and his head throbbing. There was a heavy pain in his arms and across his chest caused, he realized as he got slowly to his feet, by having slept with his fists clenched. It was like waking from a nightmare, though he had no recollection of having had one. He took some deep breaths and staggered to the bathroom to splash cold water on himself

and to try and unjumble the thoughts that were knotted
in his head. Ridiculous to get into such a state over
nothing. Of course he had informed the officer about
Signora Giusti's woman — and what a grim picture he had
conjured up of her in his half-sleep! The thought of the
tight-lipped face he had invented made him shudder as
he put on a clean shirt. He went through to the kitchen
and heated up the remains of his breakfast coffee in the
hope of waking himself up properly and clearing his
brain. He drank off the two inches of thick, scalding
coffee in one mouthful and got into his jacket; he still had
work to do. But the headache and the nightmare heavi-
ness in his chest stayed with him throughout an evening of
plodding from hotel to pensione through the still
sweltering, ice-cream-splattered streets, of going up in
lifts lined with red carpet or disfigured by graffiti, and
going down staircases smelling of new paint or stale
cooking, of reaching for the blue register in reception
halls where the scraping of cutlery in half-glimpsed
dining-rooms reminded him how late it was and how little
he had eaten all day.

'The trouble is,' said the Marshal, addressing his absent
wife, as he often did, 'I don't like the way that man died. I
don't like it at all . . . Right, that's ready for the salt.'

The last remark referred to a large pan of water which
had begun to boil furiously. He spooned the salt in and
watched it froth up and dissolve, then slid a thick fistful
of spaghetti out of their cellophane wrapping and spun
them with surprising delicacy through the bubbling
water. Of the two meals in his culinary repertoire he had
chosen spaghetti al pomodoro rather than bread and
cheese, partly because he was very hungry and partly
because it was more cheering and so worth the extra heat
that the boiling pan would cause. The night was just as
still and suffocatingly hot as the day, and there was no

point in opening windows to let in warm air and mosquitoes.

The Marshal, having got back late from his rounds, was pottering round the little kitchen, wearing his vest and a worn old pair of khaki trousers. He took from the cupboard a new jar of the tomato and herb preserve which his wife made every summer, packing the jars in a cardboard box for him to bring up to Florence on the train. It was the last jar; in August he would be going home for the holidays.

On top of the cupboard the television was switched on, but with the sound barely audible. The Marshal got more comfort and company out of the noise from upstairs where the lads were playing cards, to judge from their disjointed murmurings and occasional arguments, to the accompaniment of Gino's radio. The radio was a present from his brother and his most prized possession, though he always let the others choose the programmes.

'God, this heat!'

That was Lorenzini opening the window above the Marshal's kitchen and then shutting it again in despair.

The Marshal showered cheese on to his mountain of tomato-topped spaghetti, poured himself a small tumbler of wine and sat down at the kitchen table, gazing absently at the television. As he plunged his fork through the powdery cheese and glistening red sauce, the noise from upstairs suddenly increased. Di Nuccio's voice began to rise and fall in an anguished, almost tearful diatribe, interrupted by the cynical staccato of Lorenzini giving him a lecture in Florentine good sense. As Di Nuccio became more tearful, Lorenzini got more exasperated. Without distinguishing more than the odd word of their conversation, the Marshal knew that this signalled the end of Di Nuccio's latest love-affair, the eighth, or was it the ninth, of the last two years. The Marshal had seen them together in the piazza a week ago and had been even

more horror-stricken than usual by this girl, a skinny, unappetizing creature in skin-tight black trousers, a baggy,
shocking-pink T-shirt with glittery designs all over the
front, and a thickly painted face half buried in a mass of
frizzy, bleached hair. Watching them from across the street,
the Marshal's big eyes had almost popped out of his head
with disapproval but Di Nuccio hadn't even noticed
him, bending over the girl as he was, and talking nineteen
to the dozen. The pattern of these love-affairs always followed the same strict timetable: a month of preliminaries,
during which Di Nuccio went about like a love-sick cat,
talking about nothing else and boring everybody to tears,
then a relatively calm couple of months during which the
girl was putty in his hands, then the Obstacle. The
Obstacle varied from some mythical rival to the disapproval of *La Mamma*. Once the Obstacle was named, the
affair would break up and Di Nuccio would maintain a
morose silence for about a week.

Lorenzini, who had just applied for permission to
marry the girl he had been courting since he left school,
exhausted himself trying to talk sense to Di Nuccio. Di
Nuccio privately told the Marshal that Lorenzini was a
heartless northerner who understood nothing. The
Marshal privately explained to young Gino that Lorenzini
was a romantic who indeed understood nothing, and
that, sooner or later, when Di Nuccio had had enough
adventures to satisfy his vanity, he would find a girl-
friend who just happened to have a café or a bit of land in
the family and Love Would Find A Way. Gino contented
himself with being a good listener.

A film was starting on the television and the Marshal
reached over to turn up the volume, but before he could
do so the telephone rang. Going through to the bedroom
where he took his calls at night when the office was shut,
he thought at once of the Dutchman, realizing that this
thought had been with him all along, as if he'd been

expecting a call.

But it was his wife:

'I want the Marshal!' she shouted, never convinced that the telephone could bridge a thousand miles without some effort on her part.

'Teresa? It's me. What is it? What's wrong?'

She never phoned him except in an emergency. Normally, he phoned her on Thursday, his day off. This was Monday.

'Salvatore! Is it you? There's nothing wrong. Just something I have to ask you—Thursday would be too late.'

'Where are you? At the post office?'

'At Don Torquato's house—and he refuses to let me pay so I'll have to be quick. It's about Mamma.'

'She's not worse?'

'No different. You know the doctor said there'd be no change until . . .'

'Don't shout!'

'Can you hear me? Salva!'

'Yes. I said don't—'

'Well, listen: there's been a change in the arrangements about the summer and it looks as if Nunziata can't take her holidays in August after all . . .'

Nunziata, the Marshal's sister, lived with them and worked part-time in a plastics factory.

'But surely, if they promised . . .'

'They did promise! But full-time workers have priority, and it seems somebody else has changed and wants those two weeks—you know what that's going to mean for us . . .'

That they would get no time together with the children, no days at the beach. Without Nunziata they couldn't leave the old lady who could neither move nor speak.

'We'll manage,' he murmured, 'somehow . . .'

'Wait a minute! Can you hear me? I spoke to the district nurse and she says—can you hear me?'

'Yes, yes . . . I can . . .'

'And she says there's a possibility of getting Mamma into hospital provided we—'

'No!'

'Yes! She said if I can let her know right away—'

'No! I said no! We can't just shunt her about like a bundle of old rags.'

'Like a what?'

'Never mind. We'll manage. We'll get someone to sit with her. It's only for half the day.'

'In August?'

'We'll find somebody . . . we'll pay . . .'

'On your salary? I don't see what you've got against her going into hospital where she'll be properly looked after without paying anything . . .'

'Don't you realize? Haven't you thought that it may be the last time I see her?'

There was a moment's silence.

He could hear the pips counting away expensive seconds. At last she said, forgetting to shout:

'I was thinking of the children. You know how they look forward to the bit of time we get. I didn't mean . . .'

He had made her feel ashamed. Day after day she had to look after a very sick old lady, his mother not hers, and he had made her feel ashamed of seeming to want a few days off. If only she wouldn't ask him to decide just now. How could he explain about Signora Giusti with the seconds ticking away and the priest maybe listening? It was ridiculous, anyway . . .

'Let me think about it . . . I'll tell you on Thursday.'

'But there are so few places, if we don't . . .'

'Please. Just till Thursday.'

'All right. Salva? I didn't mean . . . Well, you're right; poor soul, it may well be her last summer. We can't deprive her of it even if she's not aware. The doctor said probably within the year, and then . . .'

'And then the three of you move up here.'

'There'll still be Nunziata . . .'

'We agreed. It'll work out—but we can't talk about it now. Don Torquato . . .'

'Oh Lord! Oh! Excuse me, Father . . . oh dear . . . I'm going! Good night! Salva, can you hear me? I'm going! Good night!'

'Good night . . .'

The line went dead.

Slowly he put down the receiver and sat down heavily on the bed. The silence closed in around him. He hadn't said one kind word to her . . . it was always so difficult on the telephone. He hadn't even asked after the boys. Now she would be apologizing profusely to Don Torquato, hurrying down the ill-lit street, wondering whether Nunziata had managed to get the boys into bed.

They put the old lady to bed at seven-thirty, she and Nunziata carrying her enormous, barely sentient body between them. At six-thirty each morning they carried her back to the sitting-room, after washing and dressing her, or sat her out on the little terrace until the sun got too hot. When Nunziata had gone to work, Teresa got the children up and then stripped the old lady's bed and began washing the soaked sheets. In the evenings she shopped while Nunziata stayed at home. That was her best time of the day.

Sometimes the old lady whined for hours on end, asking to be taken home. Nobody knew why; she had lived in that same house eleven years. But she had no idea any more of who or where she was. Teresa would go about her housework saying, 'That's enough now . . . hush.'

She was still a young woman, his wife. She needed a rest, a bit of pleasure. He knew that when she got frustrated and unhappy, instead of complaining uselessly she would throw herself into her housework, cleaning everything three times over in her fury. Then the two little boys would keep well out of the way and not dare put a foot wrong.

He couldn't phone her back. On Thursday she would be at Don Torquato's by nine o'clock, waiting for his call. There was nothing to be done till then . . . and he hadn't said a kind word . . .

Back in the kitchen, the film on television was well under way and he stared at it for some moments without bothering to turn up the sound, knowing that he hadn't the patience to try and pick up the thread of the story.

'Hmph,' he grunted, and turned it off. Perhaps, in some obscure way, he was trying to apologize to his wife by doing what she would have done, feeling oppressed as he was feeling. At any rate, he suddenly threw himself into work, splashing about with his pots in the sink. Had he been wrong to give up trying for a post down in Syracuse? It had always been assumed that that was what he would do, but then they had talked about schools for the children, opportunities . . . but his mother had been too old to move, and then the stroke . . .

When the kitchen was in order, he went through to the office, switched on the desk lamp, and began to type up his notes on the Dutchman. He typed fast, with two fingers. When he had finished, he pushed his chair back from the desk and began to read them through. The whole thing seemed as if it had happened a hundred years ago to somebody else. He shrugged, slid the papers into a buff folder and switched off the lamp. With his mind quite empty and numbed, he went to bed and fell asleep immediately.

CHAPTER 3

'Oh, Gigi! *Amore mio!*' shrieked Di Nuccio in a strangulated falsetto.

'Only yooou! can make my dreams come true . . . !'

That was Lorenzini's baritone.

'Why was he-e born so beautiful . . . !' they sang in unison, and the clumping of boots on the boards overhead finally induced the Marshal to climb the stairs, puffing, and appear in the doorway.

'Now then, now then!'

Stumbling a little, Di Nuccio and Lorenzini set Gino back on his feet and fell silent.

'Sounds more like a schoolroom than a barracks,' grumbled the Marshal, trying to look annoyed. But he couldn't help smiling at the sight before him. Gino stood between the other two, who were in rolled-up shirt sleeves and open collars, ready for a hot day's work, but Gino himself was resplendent: his khaki trousers were carefully creased, his jacket and tie immaculate, his yellow hair sprouting like a chrysanthemum, still damp from the shower. Even his collar was more or less straight beneath his shining round face.

'You get off with you, if you're going out. It's time these two were busy, it must be eight o'clock. Where are you going, anyway?'

'With my brother.' Gino's smile, which had faded into apprehensiveness on the Marshal's arrival, reappeared. School was finished for the summer and when Gino's leave started this weekend, the 'boys from Pordenone' would make the long journey north together.

'We're going round the shops for some presents to take home . . .'

The Marshal didn't ask why Gino should be going out in uniform on his day off, knowing well that they were the only decent, new clothes he had ever had. In any case, his uniforms were his one vanity, which made it all the more comical that he could never quite organize himself inside them. Winter serge or summer khaki, battle-dress or braided and feathered parade dress, they all bulged, wrinkled and popped, defying his dogged efforts to wear them worthily. Today's effort was his most successful yet, but by lunch-time he would look as though he'd been under siege for a week.

The other two clattered off downstairs to do a routine ammunition check in the store behind the Marshal's office.

'Aren't you going?'

'Yes, Marshal. But I'm going down into the piazza first to get the others some cigarettes—and we need some bread and mineral water, so if you need anything . . .'

'Always running everybody's errands. It's your free day.'

'But I don't mind going. Really.'

It was true that he got real pleasure out of every little thing he did, especially for other people.

'All right, but I don't need anything—wait, yes I do—bring me some matches, will you? I opened the last box when I made the coffee this morning.'

Gino accepted a thousand-lire note and saluted solemnly. The Marshal returned his salute and followed him, shaking his head, smilingly, down the stairs.

The report on the Dutchman was lying on the desk where he had left it last night, and he stood a moment, alone in the office, with his thick fingers resting lightly on the buff folder. The episode still seemed very remote, so much so that the Marshal felt he wanted to go round to the flat again and give the deadened images some life. It wasn't curiosity, and he was in no way duty bound to investigate the matter any further without having received orders from the officer in charge.

Perhaps it just didn't seem right that the man should be so instantly forgotten, that his death, so prolonged and painful, should be labelled a suicide and then dismissed. Had his wife been informed? Had anyone been to get more information about him from Signora Giusti? The fingers on the buff folder began to tap impatiently. After a moment he sat down, filled in the date on the daily sheet, and then took up the post that had been left out for him the evening before and at which he had only glanced before typing his report. All internal circulars . . . There were two new names on the list of wanted terrorists, both thought to be in Rome. Three names had been taken off. The Marshal took a copy of the old list out of his breast pocket, substituted the new one, and pinned a second copy on to the notice board. The phone hadn't rung. If they insisted on the suicide theory . . . but they couldn't do that, surely, or not until the autopsy report came in . . . and even then there would be formalities. Would his wife come to identify the body? He wondered now what had happened to Signora Giusti's set of keys.

When the phone still hadn't rung at nine o'clock, the Marshal stared blankly for a moment at the short-circuit television that covered the entrance to the office, showing him a gardener pointing out a way through the Boboli Gardens to a group of tourists, then he got up and prepared to go out.

'Take over at my desk,' he told Lorenzini. 'I'll do the first half of my hotel round.'

He picked up the buff file and looked at his watch.

'I should be delivering this at Headquarters at about eleven, so if you need me . . .'

'Right, sir.'

'And I'll take my car.'

Lorenzini looked surprised but said nothing. It was

true that neither the jeep nor the van were of much use on a trip when you had to find a parking space in the shade every few minutes, but usually the Marshal walked.

Driving slowly down the crowded forecourt in his Fiat 500 it occurred to him to wonder why he hadn't mentioned the Dutchman to the lads. It wasn't like him to be secretive. Afterwards, he thought it must have been because, for once in his life, he intended to stick his neck out, and hadn't wanted to involve them. But he was to need Lorenzini's help before very long, as it turned out.

Waiting at the bottom of the slope to join the traffic going by, he scowled to left and right. It was no way for a man to die, alone in a dust-sheeted house. There was something pitiful, too, in his attempt to bind up his bleeding hands when there was so much else wrong . . . But then, Signora Giusti had said he was a jeweller and goldsmith, so his hands were important to him. Or maybe he just wasn't in full possession of his senses by that time. It was no way to die, anyhow . . .

'What's the matter with you? Marshall'

It was the car park attendant who had saluted him, saying good-morning and waving him out, receiving nothing for his pains but a gloomy stare. Well, there was no time to explain. The Marshal nodded briefly to him and drove away, leaving the attendant staring after him and muttering:

'What a face . . .'

'It seems, anyway, as if we're finally getting somewhere.'

'It's usually a question of patience and routine,' offered the Marshal politely.

'Quite. Even so, with two deaths in three weeks we've had to step things up . . .'

Most of what the Marshal knew about the case he had read in the paper, although he had received a notice about it from the drug squad and been asked to keep an eye open for certain signs. It all started when it was noticed that the usual places where heroin was distributed and injected were being used less and less, and a systematic check throughout the city had revealed no new centre, which could only mean that some indoor place had been set up and was doing good business.

Then, one night, a boy of eighteen had been found dead, not of an overdose but of blood poisoning. He had been found many hours after his death in a public square where he would have been spotted immediately during the daylight hours when he had died. Somebody had certainly dumped him. It was a very young, plain-clothes man who, making the round of all the dead boy's friends and haunts on the pretext of looking for a fix, had found the place whose existence the drug squad had so long suspected. It was in a condemned *palazzo* with no running water or electricity, but in its sordid way it was well equipped. There was a large supply of heroin and cocaine, a drawer full of new hypodermics from the supermarket, and a filthy bin full of bloody, used ones. There were pharmacist's scales, a purpose-made burner, and even styptic pencils. The big dusty room had six beds on which, having paid between thirty thousand to fifty thousand lire inclusive, the customer could lie down until the flash effect was over.

The second death brought in men from homicide to assist the drug squad in their manpower-consuming surveillance of the 'hotel' and its proprietors. The arrests were imminent.

'What's really incredible,' the young Lieutenant continued, 'is that there haven't been more deaths. They're cutting the heroin with whitewash scraped off the walls of this filthy den!'

The Marshal murmured something suitable, wondering how on earth he could bring up the Dutchman business if the officer didn't mention it first. In the end he simply

indicated the buff file that was lying on the desk between
them.

'Ah, the Dutchman, isn't it? You brought it over
specially?'

'I was passing,' lied the Marshal noncommittally.

'Of course. Yes . . .'

He had opened the file and was scanning its contents.

'You're a friend of the old lady, I remember . . . and
that's how you came to discover . . .'

He fell silent, reading.

The Marshal did not contradict him. There was a
framed photograph of the Commander-in-chief on the
wall, and a small crucifix, so he stared at those. Every few
seconds, the door across the corridor opened, and a noise
like that of a beehive swelled out from the operations
room, stopping abruptly as the door closed again.

'Hm.' The Lieutenant looked up. 'We've managed to
contact his wife.'

'But you didn't say you thought—'

'That it was suicide? No, of course not. The autopsy
report should be in this afternoon—we asked for priority
under the circumstances. They will probably want to take
the body home for burial, and in this heat . . . well, we
don't want a repeat of the exploding coffin episode.
Unfortunately the young woman is expecting her first
child very shortly. We must do our best to deal with everything as smoothly and as quickly as possible.'

'A funny time to choose . . .'

'I beg your pardon?'

'A funny time to choose to commit suicide. *He* was expecting his first child, too.'

'Other considerations must have been stronger.'

'They must have been very strong indeed if they were
stronger than that.'

'Listen, Marshal, I can see from this report that you
don't think he committed suicide, but in fact he

quarrelled with his wife and his mother-in-law before he left. I understand that this was supposed to be a business trip he was making and that both women suspected it was unnecessary and objected to his leaving home with his wife's pregnancy so advanced. He may well have felt remorse.'

'Yes, sir. Funny he didn't catch a train . . .'

'A train?'

'A train back to Amsterdam, sir, and go home. If he felt remorse . . .'

The young officer was not amused. The Marshal went on, avoiding his eyes:

'Forgive me, Lieutenant. It's just, as you say, that I'm taking rather a personal interest in the matter, as a . . . a friend of the old lady, Signora Giusti. Suicide is a hard burden to bear for those who are left behind.'

'And you think this burden would be lessened by our telling this young, pregnant wife that we think he had a woman in the flat with him? You think that would make his trip to Florence more palatable to her?'

'To be honest,' admitted the Marshal, 'I hadn't thought of that . . .'

Why hadn't he? He realized that, for him, the woman in the flat just didn't have that significance because . . . because he had thought of her all along as an *old* woman, as the face he had invented in his dream. What was there in Signora Giusti's account that would explain that? Nothing that he could offer as an explanation now, at any rate.

'You know,' said the officer more gently, seeing the Marshal's confusion, 'murderers don't attack people with sleeping pills. Sleeping pills usually mean suicide or an accident. And if it's at all possible, we'll set this down as the latter.'

'It's usually women, though, isn't it?'

'Women?'

'Who use sleeping pills to commit suicide. Men tend to choose a more active, violent method . . . the river, a high building, a razor . . .'

His eyes rolled quickly across the officer's face and away again. That's better, he was thinking, I've got him worried now, at least.

'That's true,' the officer admitted.

After a pause he went on: 'There's one thing that bothers me, I don't mind telling you, and that's his clothes . . .'

The Marshal was almost holding his breath.

'The clothes in his suitcase, I mean, not the ones he was wearing. There was a dark suit, quite unsuitable for this time of year, and a black tie . . . as if he were here for a funeral. His wife couldn't enlighten us because, after the quarrel, he did his own packing. It doesn't make your woman theory any more likely, I must say . . . Of course, if there was a woman it could just have been a prostitute, given that he was alone in the city . . .'

'I'll inquire,' offered the Marshal quietly, watching the other's face.

What would he say? Only the Substitute Prosecutor could order the scope of this inquiry to be widened. The Marshal devoutly wished that this officer were not so young, so obviously inexperienced. In these cases it was always better if nothing had to be said. Although an officer had no power to change the direction of an inquiry, should any information come to light in the course of routine duties, he could take action on it.

The Lieutenant was still thinking it over. Perhaps he needed a little help.

'Nothing we can really do, of course,' said the Marshal, rising, 'unless the Substitute Prosecutor decides there's a case to answer, but I'll just keep an eye open on my usual rounds and if I find anything interesting I'll let you know . . .'

'Yes, do.'

The young man was evidently relieved. But it was better that way, the Marshal reflected as he left the room with a salute, because he may have been convinced for the moment but it wasn't a conviction that would stand up to even one scathing remark from the Substitute Prosecutor. He'd be a fool to stick his neck out publicly without a scrap of real evidence, and up to now there wasn't a scrap of evidence, or even a witness . . . let alone a suspect!

'I wonder how right I was,' he mumbled, repeatedly banging his car door as he always had to do to make it shut, 'about a man not using sleeping pills to commit suicide. Who would know . . . ?'

'Yesterday at about two o'clock. I'm afraid I can't be more exact about the time.'

The long, dark-tiled room with its ecclesiastical white walls and grey and white striped vaulting was dim and gratefully cool, and the Marshal was glad to take off his hat and sunglasses.

'That's all right. The call slip will have the exact time on it along with the name and address — excuse me a moment . . .'

One of the seven telephones on the desk was ringing, and the Servant, a solemn, middle-aged man in morning suit and white tie, picked up the receiver and spoke quietly into it.

'And the address? Yes, immediately, don't worry. Stay with her and try to keep her calm . . .'

He pressed the emergency bell and stepped down from the glass-enclosed platform where his desk stood.

Two steps away was a long mahogany bench on which a huge ledger lay open under a wrought-iron lamp. By the time the Servant reached the ledger, two dozen Brothers had appeared before it and were waiting in silence. The

Servant read out four names and then handed the call slip to the most senior of them. The four pulled on their hoods and went quickly out to where the ambulance driver had already started his engine on hearing the bell. As the siren started up and then faded into the distance, the rest of the Brothers dispersed to benches in dim corners and resumed their newspapers or quiet conversations. The only sound had been the rustle and click of their black gowns. The whole operation was over in much less than a minute.

The Marshal, who had been calling out the *Misericordia* for years without giving them much conscious thought, was impressed.

'Very efficient,' he murmured.

'We've been practising,' the Servant reminded him, with just a hint of a complacent smile, 'for a good seven hundred years. Now . . . two o'clockish, you said . . . Here we are.'

He took out the call slip and turned back a page in the ledger, running his finger down the signatures.

'I hope I'm not breaking any rules . . .' The Marshal was turning his hat round and round in his hands. 'I'm not a Florentine myself so I don't know all that much . . .'

'Don't worry. Anonymity is the ideal where charitable work's concerned, but in a case like this . . . Here we are: Piazza Santo Spirito, I remember the call — in fact, I'm glad you got in touch with us because we were wondering . . . the man died and there seem to have been no members of the family there so that we couldn't ask if there was money needed . . .'

'You can help in cases like that?'

'Certainly, if there's need.'

'In this case money isn't a problem.' But he made a mental note to come and see them about Signora Giusti. 'The problem is whether he committed suicide.'

The Servant looked up. 'That's a heavy accusation to make.'

'I think so, too. That's why I'd like the opinion of the Brothers who were there. The only suicides I've dealt with have been the people the fire brigade fish out of the Arno. This is very different.'

'I understand.'

He looked again at the ledger. 'But I'm afraid you won't find them here today. Most people only do one hour a week. With fourteen thousand of us there's no need for them to do more and most of them are working men. I'll give you the names and addresses of three of them, the new boy won't be able to help you . . .'

The telephone rang before he could write them down.

'Here . . . perhaps you could do it—these three.'

He reached for the red telephone which was a direct line to Police Headquarters:

'*Misericordia* . . . yes . . . the angle of Via Martelli and . . . ?'

On the steps outside, the Marshal paused to put on his sunglasses and look at the three addresses in his notebook. Across the road, beyond the row of ambulances, tourists were swarming in the shade around the base of the octagonal blue and white Baptistry, and the Cathedral bell was ringing the Angelus, reminding him that he had better get back to Pitti. The lads would soon be back from the mensa with the lunches stacked in the back of the van.

'*Suicide* . . . ? I'm sorry—do sit down. Martha! What about bringing another cup for the Marshal?'

'No, no . . . there's no need, really . . . I've already had . . .'

'I'm having one myself so you'll join me. One coffee a day is all I ever have. In the mornings I find it too strong, I take tea, and after supper it would keep me awake. You have a cup with me now and it'll do you no harm. You've eaten?'

'Yes, but I've had . . .'

'Right then. Two coffees. Here we are. Sugar?'

'A little. You're a Florentine?'

An unnecessary question with just a hint of irony in it, for the Marshal was quite used, by this time, to being ordered about by a wagging finger, and to sentences that began 'That's as may be, but we Florentines . . .'

'Florentine? Three hundred years my family has lived in this street. Have a bit more sugar, it'll be too bitter like that.'

'I don't . . .'

'There. Now, what were you wanting to ask me—I don't want to be rude but, the thing is, I'm not one of those that takes a four-hour lunch-break, even in the summer; two hours is plenty for me because I don't sleep. It's my nerves.'

'Or the coffee?' the Marshal couldn't resist saying.

'How do you mean?'

'Nothing, nothing. All I want is your opinion. You were the senior Brother on that call?'

'That's right. I joined during the war when I was sixteen, nineteen-forty, that was, and then, of course, I was called up two years after that. Bad days, those were. Young ones today have no idea. I started work for my father as a printer's apprentice at age twelve, right here in this building—not that I regret it, I don't hold with all this staying at school until you're twenty; it's too late to start learning anything by the time they get out. I was a qualified printer by that age. The trouble with Italy—'

'I know,' said the Marshal. 'Nobody can find an apprentice anymore, and when you find one they have to be paid a full wage right away when they can't do anything, not to mention insurance . . .'

He hoped this précis would dispose of what would

otherwise be a two-hour discussion.

'What I'd like your opinion on is the death of that Dutchman, Goossens, his name was, and like yourself he was a craftsman. The Substitute Prosecutor seems inclined to set it down as a suicide, as I said . . .'

'*Suicide*?' said the printer again, shaking his head and tutting knowledgeably. 'No no no no no.'

'You must have attended a number of suicides over the years, I suppose?'

'A fair number, yes, but never one that looked anything like that.'

'You think there may have been foul play?'

'I'm not saying that. It had the look of an accident, in some ways, as if he'd taken something by mistake and then gone rushing about trying to remedy it, cutting his hands and so on. But really, I should have thought the autopsy would tell you more than I could in that line.'

'Yes, of course, but given that it's an odd case, I wanted to know what you thought.'

He didn't say that he was unlikely ever to see the autopsy report.

'Have you ever known a man to commit suicide with sleeping pills?'

'Once. Oddly enough it wasn't on a *Misericordia* call, he was a neighbour of ours, a cobbler. Even so, when he'd taken the pills he put a polythene bag over his head, to make sure. It was after the flood, you know, and he'd lost everything, absolutely everything; his shop was on the ground floor and he lived behind it — we suffered a lot of damage ourselves, down in the workshop, but at least we were all right up here. There was compensation, of course, we got new equipment throughout, but old chaps like that who had worked alone all their lives, they just couldn't believe that anybody would help them, and so . . . Anyway, old Querci killed himself, and he used sleeping pills perhaps because the family he was staying with got them for him to try and calm him down, but more likely because he hadn't a tool left in the world with which to harm himself. To tell you the truth, in the case of the Dutchman yesterday, it was something very simple that made me think it was an accident; he was dressed, you see . . .'

'Yes, he was . . .'

'And fully dressed, with his tie properly tied. He'd put his slippers on, but otherwise . . . Somehow it's natural, if you're going to die in your sleep, to go to bed — even if he took an accidental overdose it means he must have been going to bed. But there he was fully dressed, and the bed wasn't even made up. He didn't live there, they say?'

'Who says?'

'The paper. There was a couple of lines about it this morning.'

He picked up the newspaper from beside his coffee cup, and put on a pair of dark-rimmed spectacles.

'Here: "A man found dying of an overdose of sleeping pills in a fourth-floor flat in Piazzo Santo Spirito was identified as Ton Goossens, a businessman from Amsterdam. The body was taken to the Medico-Legal Institute for a post-mortem." '

Nothing else. No journalists had turned up at the time so they must have got their information from Headquarters, along with the daily quota of handbag snatches and road accidents.

'We always look for the bottle, you know,' the printer said, folding up the newspaper, 'because we have to take it with us to the hospital or the morgue.'

'The bottle . . . the bottle that contained the sleeping pills?'

'Exactly. We didn't find one in this case . . . Of course, your people were still there when we left.'

'I rather think that they didn't find one, either — though it could be amongst the broken glass they collected from the bathroom.'

'Well, once you know what the drug was . . . But, you know, the technical cause of death is probably going to be heart failure, don't you think so? And if he turns out to have been known to have a heart problem, whether he took the drugs on purpose or not, it would be kinder to his family . . . He did have a family?'

'Yes. He had a wife who's expecting a baby any day now. And a stepmother.'

'Expecting a baby? Poor creature . . .'

'Dreadful tragedy,' said the young Count softly, with the slight lisp peculiar to his class. 'The trouble is, all our servants are in the country so I don't know what I can offer you . . . let me see . . . oh dear, not even a coffee . . .'

The Marshal blinked with relief.

'A little drop of vinsanto, yes . . .'

'No, really . . .'

But the Count was on his feet and rambling away in the direction of some distant dining-room.

The Marshal sighed. He'd had another coffee, his third, plus a large ice-cream, forced down him by the second Brother he had visited, who owned a bar where they made their own ice-cream and where it would have been taken as an insult had he refused to try it.

He sat, holding his hat, on the edge of a dust-sheeted and very hard chair, surrounded by a sea of miscellaneous white-shrouded shapes, like someone marooned on an ice-floe, staring out of the enormous window at an unaccustomed view of the city. It was spread out below him, a noiseless, dreamlike tapestry of mellow terracotta out of which rose confections of blue and white marble whose gilded decorations reflected the low sun. The river, where it was visible, was dissolving from olive to gold in the evening light. Only a couple of hours ago, the Marshal had talked of fishing desperate citizens out of that same water that lay there smooth as oil, and every day that week the paper had carried letters suggesting ways of controlling the increasing population of rats . . .

The vision was framed by long, sweeping curtains of faded blue silk. Looking more closely, the Marshal saw that what appeared to be a pattern of darker horizontal stripes was caused by the silk having rotted with old age.

'Beautiful, isn't it?' The Count was back, carrying a silver tray with a bottle and two dusty glasses on it. He looked about him, trying to decide which of the ghostly shapes might be some sort of table, eventually placing the tray on the broad wooden step running along beneath the window.

'We have one of the best views in Florence. I like the country well enough but I'd as soon stay here all summer if my father didn't insist we all go . . . You're very lucky to have found me, you know, because I only came down to collect some more books. I read a great deal in the country. Here you are, try this. It's from our own vine-yards but we make so little of it that we never sell any . . .'

'Very nice,' murmured the Marshal, sipping a little un-happily at the dusty rim but appreciating the dryness of the liqueur wine that was so often stickily sweet. He wondered where he could put his glass down, and eventually decided to keep hold of it, balancing his hat on one knee to make room.

'This is not, as I said before, an official call exactly. I'm just trying to satisfy myself in my own mind as to what happened . . .' The Marshal was sweating a little, and his free hand groped for a handkerchief in his trouser pocket. He had no right to be here, and if, however inadvertently, he annoyed this young man who looked so blandly pleased to see him, it would only take a brief telephone call . . .

'I just thought your experience as a Brother of the *Misericordia* might help me . . .'

'Yes yes yes . . . but of course I'm not a Brother, not yet . . . But you're not a Florentine.'

He had noticed that the Marshal looked baffled.

'I understand.' His tone implied that it could happen to anybody; just bad luck. 'There are only seventy-two Brothers, as there were originally: twelve prelates, twenty priests, twelve nobles, and twenty-eight artists. The rest of us are only assistant brothers, really. My father thought I ought not . . . he's one of the twelve nobles, as I shall be, eventually . . . but I wanted to join as soon as I could. It's a great tradition, you know . . . and then, one can talk to the other Brothers. While we're waiting for calls. I've had a number of interesting conversations . . . I like to meet people, don't you?'

The Marshal was too bemused to think of an answer, but he noticed, when the young man bent down to refill their glasses, that he was balding a little on his crown. He wore a pair of worn-out slacks like the Marshal used for pottering in the kitchen, and the childish striped T-shirt, buttoned up at the collar, was much too small for him.

'No, no . . . that's plenty.'

The Marshal tried to withdraw his glass, his eyes still rolling over the young man's clothes. The shoes looked odd, being black, city shoes, some sort of absent-minded concession to the idea of dressing to come into town? Surely not; perhaps he changed when he got here. How old would he be? Much older than the Marshal had first thought when judging by the T-shirt and the childlike facial expression. Probably nearer forty than thirty . . . He was still talking, barely pausing to draw breath.

'There's my sister, of course, but once we're out in the country she thinks of nothing but her horses, and I've never been strong enough . . .'

He was certainly too thin and very pale. The Marshal thought briefly of the escaped prisoner at the Pensione Giulia . . . was it only yesterday? His complexion had given him away . . .

The thing was, to get the talk back to the subject in

hand. But the Marshal was reluctant to ask outright. He knew from experience that the phrasing of a question suggests the required answer, and he wanted an unbiased opinion.

'It's conversation that I like, and friends. Friends are very important. That's one of the reasons why I enjoyed school so much, despite the trouble I had with mathematics. Italian was my great subject. I remember Padre Begnini saying once . . .'

Although the evening outside was still bright and rosy, the light was fading in the vast room, making the shrouded furniture look even more ghostly. The high ceiling was a traditional Florentine one in dark wood, divided into deep-set squares, each with a carved red and gold rosette in the centre.

'I see you're admiring the ceiling. My mother prefers the frescoed ones on the next floor, they're supposed to be by Bonechi, but I like the wooden ceilings best. You see, I admire first-class craftsmanship more than third-rate art.'

'The man who died was a craftsman. The man you attended yesterday.'

'He was? Oh dear, and you wanted to talk about him, while here am I leading the conversation on to other things. You'll be thinking I'm the culprit!'

'The culprit?'

'I was only joking. *Of course, I have a perfect alibi!*'

He made the last remark in English, and then began to laugh, an uncontrolled, high-pitched giggle.

'Forgive me,' he said at last, misinterpreting the Marshal's frown of incomprehension for one of disapproval. 'These are serious matters, grave matters, I know that. I've prayed for him, too, and for whoever did it.'

The Marshal's face remained expressionless, but his big eyes were fixed on the Count's as he spoke.

'What makes you think someone else did it? Rather, I mean, than that he wanted to kill himself?'

'But . . . well, he said, didn't he? I know he didn't say who did it, but he was trying to tell us that somebody or other didn't do it, surely you heard? He said, "It wasn't her." Naturally, one thought . . .'

Naturally. He could have been rambling, of course, thinking of something completely remote from his own death . . . and yet, he had just spoken to Signora Giusti, as if he were quite aware of where he was. The Marshal admitted to himself that he wouldn't have made much of a detective. He had heard the Dutchman's remark, all right, but he hadn't wanted to interpret it that way because it seemed to discount the only person known to have been—or thought to have been—in the flat with him; seemed, as everyone else was inclined to agree, including the Substitute Prosecutor, to point either to suicide or an accident by absolving the only person who might come to be accused. He might even have been absolving his wife from blame, since they had quarrelled.

'It doesn't seem likely,' the Marshal said aloud, 'that if someone had tried to murder him he would have wasted his last breath telling us who didn't do it . . .'

'It may have been important to him to save someone from unjust suspicion.'

'Or he may have been lying.'

'On his deathbed!' The young Count was shocked.

'Perhaps you're right. Did anything else strike you, apart from his words?'

'His poor hands.' He clasped his own together tightly, as if to stem some imaginary bleeding. 'But mostly his words. I suppose, now you mention it, it was odd that he should only say who it wasn't, not very helpful . . . but I wasn't struck by it at the time. What struck me most at the time was that he sounded so surprised.'

CHAPTER 4

The Marshal had a bottle of vinsanto which he laid carefully on the back seat of his car next to the beribboned parcel of cakes that had been pressed on him by the bar owner, and a copy of *The Beauties of Florence* which had been presented to him by the printer as they came out through the storeroom between stacks of cut paper where strong smells of ink and metal and a rhythmic swish and clack of machinery came from behind frosted glass panelling.

'We printed it here so they sent me a few copies—take it, take it! No compliments! You can take it back to Sicily to show your family. Sicily's beautiful, too, I don't doubt it, I don't doubt it, but Florence . . .'

The young Count's farewells had been less exuberant, despite the present of the vinsanto.

'You might want to talk to me again,' he had said hopefully.

'I don't think . . .'

'You mustn't think that because we're in the country you can't reach me. If it's something important, my father—I'll tell you what I'll do, I'll come down tomorrow, just in case you need to talk to me. I'll be here all afternoon . . . they wouldn't like it if I weren't there for lunch, you understand, but I can say that you might want to see me sometime in the afternoon? I could say that?'

'Yes, I suppose you could say that . . .'

All down the marble hallway, there had been half-moon tables with gilded lamps on them, alternating with elaborately carved oak chairs. Some of the rooms they had passed through were almost empty of furniture. They had passed a small, concealed door let into the wall on

the left, and the Marshal had time to glimpse a single bed
with a dark blue linen suit thrown across it before the
Count hurriedly shut the door.

'I'll leave you here.'

The Marshal had been out on the first-floor landing
when the Count made this abrupt remark.

'Then, goodbye and thank you . . .'

But by the time he turned, the door had shut and he
was alone.

There were still two hotels to be visited. The Marshal
was tired and not at all sure, thinking about it as he drove
along by the river, whether his visits to the Brothers had
been useful or not. They hadn't turned up any concrete
facts that he could present to an officer, and the Brothers
of the *Misericordia*, although acceptable as reliable and
experienced witnesses, were not officially expert ones.
And the expert ones weren't going to give their findings to
him. Unless . . .

The Marshal pulled up at a bar, went in and asked for
a telephone token. If there was one thing his last visit had
done it was to make him more determined. Perhaps it
had been the deserted-looking room with its dust-sheeted
furniture which had brought the deadened images to life.
After all, if somebody did kill the Dutchman, what a
cold-blooded, sinister killing it had been. The meeting
must have been arranged since the man only went there
once or twice a year, and nobody goes about carrying
enormous doses of sleeping pills . . .

Waiting for the token, he glared about him at the
milling tourists buying ice-cream and evening apéritifs.
Somewhere in the city . . . it could be any of these people;
anyone . . . dressed like any other holidaymaker . . .

A middle-aged German couple, unnerved by the
hostile glare discernible even behind his dark glasses, left
their drinks unfinished and hurried out.

'Is something the matter?' asked the barman, handing

over the token.

'What? What should be the matter?' growled the Marshal. He paid and strode to the telephone.

The barman looked apprehensively after him and then at his waiter, who shrugged. 'None of our business, I suppose . . .'

'Let's hope not. I don't want any shoot-outs with terrorists taking place in my bar, thanks.'

And he, too, began to scan the innocent-looking tourists.

'Rubbish! That sort of thing only happens in Rome . . .'

But both of them touched the metal edge of the counter to ward off evil, and the barman, dropping ice-cubes into three Camparis for an outside table, kept an eye on the Marshal's broad back.

'Di Nuccio? What? I can't hear, this place is packed . . . Well, get what details you can and send them over with the daily sheet—Lorenzini will have to sign it, I'm going to be late . . . I shall be at the Medico-Legal Institute and then . . . let me see, the Pensione Annamaria and the Albergo del Giardino, those are my last two. If I'm not back—and I don't think I will be—you'll have to stay in, or if you want to eat at the mensa, go in relays. Don't leave Gino in on his own, he's too young to cope. Anything else? Till later, then . . .'

He drove fast out to Careggi. The traffic was already thinning slightly with the advance of summer. By August there would only be the tourists and the people who serviced them left in the city. Out on the wide avenues the trees were tinged with gold in the evening light, the sky slightly pink.

The hospital city was an almost self-contained world with its own rhythms. There was a large and busy roundabout in the centre where kiosks sold newspapers, flowers and fruit, and signs pointed out the road to take to the different hospitals, clinics and convalescent homes and to the various specialist centres. Streams of people were going in the main doors of almost all the hospitals, carrying paper-wrapped flowers.

The Medico-Legal Institute forms part of the School of Medicine of the University of Florence, and it was at the main entrance used by students that the Marshal parked his car, avoiding the wing that housed the police laboratories and its adjacent car park. Inside, a broad tiled corridor led to the viewing rooms and the main lecture theatre. The place was deserted except for the porter's lodge where a grey head came into view above a newspaper.

'What can I do for you?' Then he spotted the Marshal's uniform. 'Go out the front door again, round the block, second on your left.'

'Actually, I was hoping for a word with Professor Forli, if he's still about.'

'He's still here. Rarely leaves before nine.' He turned to his switchboard. 'What name shall I give?'

'No! There's no need to disturb him . . . nothing urgent, you know. I'll wait a while and if he comes out I'll have a word. If not, it'll do some other time. I wouldn't want to disturb him if he's busy . . .'

'He's that all right. Rush job on this morning and then all these drug deaths . . .'

'Well, I'll wait a bit.'

'Suit yourself.'

Was the rush job the Dutchman? It was more than likely. And where would he be now in this great building . . . lying in some bleak, refrigerated compartment with his abdomen perfunctorily sewn back together . . . ?

It reminded the Marshal of the slide lecture long ago in training school when they had had to look at road accidents. He hadn't fainted but the boy next to him had. All of them had felt ill for the rest of the day and no one had touched the slightly congealed lasagne that had been served up for lunch.

How would he broach the reason for his visit to the Professor, if and when he appeared? He had no clear idea. He only knew that once the Professor got talking it was almost impossible to stop him; he was famous for it. The only problem, the Marshal mused as he wandered along the marble corridor, was to get him started before he thought to ask who the Marshal was and why he should be there.

It turned out not to be a problem at all.

The Professor came into view, striding down the corridor with the jacket of his white linen suit slung round his shoulders and a briefcase in his hand. The Marshal had no opportunity to open his mouth; the Professor called out as soon as he spotted him:

'It's already gone, if it's the Dutchman you're here for! You asked for priority and got it, despite the fact that I've got another drug death and two road accidents on my hands, and we're short staffed as usual . . .'

When he reached the Marshal he said: 'Surely it was one of your own men who collected it shortly after I telephoned . . .' He made to go and check with the porter, but the Marshal put in quickly:

'Yes, no problem, I'm sure they did—I've been out all afternoon and was going back this way so I called just in case it hadn't gone. I'm obviously out of touch. It doesn't matter . . .'

'Interesting case, very interesting. Did it myself with one or two promising students—kept them awake, plenty to think about. One of them was on to it right away. Got the connection as soon as we'd established the time of death and the stomach contents. Heart business complicated it, naturally, kept them guessing. Now the *first* thing to look for in a case of this sort . . .'

The Marshal hadn't misjudged his man. The Professor's severe good looks and almost excessive sartorial elegance gave him an aloof appearance totally at odds with his true character. He was a born teacher who, once he began to expound some theory, went ahead like a steam engine. They had been walking along the corridor towards the exit but now, every two or three steps, the Professor stopped to bombard the Marshal with technical information, nose to nose, and to fire questions at him which he then answered himself.

'*Now*! You've established the amount of barbiturate absorbed into the bloodstream. You've established the contents of the vomit containing food *and* coffee *and* barbiturate *but the stomach contains coffee and barbiturate only*! And *that* has only got as far as the duodenum. What's that telling you?'

'I . . .'

'It's telling you that there were two doses, the first dose following immediately on a meal. He's had ham, he's had bread, he's had gorgonzola, he's had a peach. He's then had coffee. The coffee contains the barbiturate. He absorbs some of it. He digests part of his meal. Then he vomits. Why?'

'I don't know . . .' The Marshal wasn't far from vomiting himself; there was a faint odour of formaldehyde in the corridor. They had turned and were walking in again.

'Because the dose is too big! People talk very glibly about neurotic women taking just so many sleeping pills, enough to create a fuss but not to kill themselves — even a doctor would have some difficulty judging a dose like that, or, if it comes to that, a dose that would surely kill. Why would he?'

'I . . .'

'Reason number one, the individual organism, that has to be taken into account; reason number two, tolerance, and this is where most suicide attempts go wrong. Drugs, many drugs, upset the stomach. Take a massive dose of sleeping pills and what happens? An hour later, or even less, you vomit the lot and you're back to square one—that's if you don't drown in your own vomit which our man came very near to doing, there were slight traces of vomit in his lungs. Three: habit. Someone who regularly takes sleeping pills is likely to make a success of the job by taking a large-ish dose of a drug she and her stomach are used to, combined with alcohol.'

The Professor strode ahead and then spun round dramatically, smacking the palm of his left hand with his right index finger.

'Now, what do we know about our Dutchman, eh?'

This time he didn't even wait for the Marshal's confused mumble but began immediately counting off points of information on his fingers.

'He's in good general health, we've seen that; the problem with his heart's a plumbing fault, not electrical. Weakened valves probably caused by a fever in childhood. Liver sound as a bell, he didn't drink much. Lungs fine, he smoked now and again but not much. He exercised, outdoors. His job was an indoor one but his skin's healthy, he's had plenty of fresh air and his muscles are in good tone despite his job being largely sedentary. Now what *is* his job?'

'He was a—'

'Where's the first place you're going to look for information?'

'His hands . . .' ventured the Marshal, remembering the young Count's words: *They must have been important to him.*

'Well done! Right! Good! He's a craftsman. He uses small metal tools regularly and he works with precious metals. He's a watchmaker or he's a silversmith or jeweller. Your lab tells me they found traces of diamond dust under his cuticles. I found tiny burns just above his wrists, the sort your wife gets when she's careless taking things out of the oven. We find faint scars of earlier burns all of the same shape and all more or less in the same place. So he's not a watchmaker, is he?'

'He's not . . . ?'

'Obviously not. He's a silversmith, a jeweller, and one with plenty of business—he has a smelting kiln or an enamelling kiln maybe, and he's loading it again before it's anywhere near cool. Asbestos gloves protect his hands, of course, but he's catching himself each time just above the wrists on the lower front bricks. Right?'

'Well I'll be damned . . .' murmured the Marshal, quite forgetting himself.

'In a city full of artisans, it's no problem distinguishing those things, but let's look at this particular jeweller: he's prosperous, he's doing well; the clothes we sent over to your lab were good clothes, his socks were silk, so was his shirt. He hardly drinks, which is saying something for a northerner, he doesn't smoke too much, he's married, wears a ring, and happily married, carries a photograph of his wife; his heart trouble's not that serious, he only knows it as a murmur he's had for years, if it deteriorates as he gets older he can have a plastic valve fitted, but it's not likely because he looks after himself. He's a happy, generally healthy, prosperous man, a craftsman who does satisfying work that he likes so much that he goes on working when he could probably just run the business and let others do the work. He takes plenty of exercise. He's no sort of candidate for sleeping pills. Right?'

'Yes,' said the Marshal, 'that's just what I felt . . .'

'*So what's wrong with him?*'

The Marshal was stunned. 'What's . . . but nothing . . .'

'But there was! Remember his hands!'

'The cuts? But surely he didn't deliberately . . .'

'Cuts, cuts! That comes later. His fingers. His fingers don't match his lungs. His lungs tell me he smokes an occasional cigarette, or even a cigar, to be sociable in company. But his fingers were deep yellow with nicotine! The fingers of the right hand, all of it new, nothing ingrained. He'd been chain-smoking for hours before he died. Yet his lungs are barely touched. My guess is that he was lighting up one cigarette after another out of nervousness and letting them burn away in his hand. Something was worrying him.'

'He'd quarrelled with his wife,' the Marshal admitted. 'She didn't want him to make this trip. She's going to have a baby soon. But what I thought was, if it bothered him so much, why not go home? He's not going to kill himself for that.'

They had come back out to the main doors and now they absent-mindedly turned and started back along the broad corridor.

'Of course, it depends,' said the Professor, frowning, 'what the trip was for. I mean, your problem may well be that, not the wife.'

'I heard it was a business trip . . .'

'In that case, I suppose you'll be looking for whoever he did business with.'

'Do you think he killed himself?'

'Strictly speaking, he died of heart failure. That's what I put in the report. It's not for me to make judicial pronouncements, and if the young woman's pregnant . . .'

'It's not for me, either, to make pronouncements; I just wanted to know what you thought. Those wounds in his hands . . . he tried to bind them up . . . they were important to him, his hands, being a craftsman.'

'I follow you. If he'd intended to die, it would hardly have mattered. But, you know, he may well have been totally confused at that stage. He'd still be very groggy from the first dose. There *are* anomalies, I agree. He took the first dose immediately after his meal—and that I don't like. I understand he'd just arrived here and so must have bought the food he ate, probably on the way from the station. He must have gone to two shops, one for the cheese, ham, coffee and bread, and another for the peaches . . .'

It brought back the previous morning vividly: the almost deserted market, the pungent odour of basil and ripe tomatoes, the cheerful stallholder in his big green apron reaching for the large peaches in their grassy tray . . .

'Now, your suicide is a self-abusing sort of person. A person who's obsessed with himself, punishes himself when things go wrong—or abuses his own body to punish someone else. He's likely to have a history of self-neglect, or of excessive fatidiousness, and an unbalanced attitude to food. This man, on the other hand, chose himself a very nice meal, visiting two shops to do it, despite, presumably, being rather tired after a long journey. Anyway, to continue to reconstruct the thing as I see it: he eats, and eats well. He then drinks coffee—not the Italian coffee which he bought, but Viennese coffee of which your people apparently found no further trace in the house—we'll come to that problem in a moment. Having drunk the coffee *with the barbiturate dissolved in it,* anomaly number three—why bother?—he then doesn't go to bed, anomaly number four—does he want to die on his feet with all his clothes on? Shortly afterwards he gets sick. He staggers to the bathroom, turns on the tap and starts vomiting. That's normal. He's already absorbed plenty of the stuff and he hangs there over the sink feeling wretched until he falls asleep with his head in his own vomit. That's normal. The sink blocks and fills up. He wakes up, choking. That's normal, though he could just as easily have drowned. Then he starts ransacking the bathroom cabinet, tumbling out every old bottle of medicine in there. Why does he do that? He was covered in ancient cough medicine and hair oil. What's he looking for?'

'I don't know . . .'

'I do. Never get so fascinated by the extraordinary that you miss the ordinary. I tell my students that every time but ninety-nine per cent of them will never learn to obey that simple rule.'

'No,' agreed the Marshal, 'they won't. It's too dull.' But it was his golden rule, too.

'Two aspirins!' announced the Professor, stopping in his tracks abruptly. 'I say two; it might have been three, but I doubt if it was more. Traces in the stomach lining and in the vomit, taken at the same time as the coffee and the first massive dose of barbiturate! And when he's been sick, confused and doped as he is, he starts scrabbling through the medicine cabinet, smashing everything in sight. What does that tell you?'

'It tells me,' said the Marshal, a trifle grumpily, 'what I already knew. He didn't know about the barbiturate. I suppose if he'd been smoking too much, and after the journey, too, he had a headache and took some aspirin from the bathroom cabinet . . .'

'And then he got sick, very sick, he realized he was doped.'

'So he thought he'd poisoned himself, that the aspirin wasn't aspirin, and he'd no idea what it might be. And his phone wasn't connected so he couldn't call for help . . .'

'I should think, anyway, that he was barely *compos mentis* at that point,' said the Professor. 'He could hardly stand; there were cuts on his knees which indicate that he must have fallen a number of times in the bathroom among all that broken glass where he lost one of his slippers, according to my assistant, and then again in the kitchen where he spilled all the coffee he'd bought.'

'Why that . . . ?'

'He was no fool. He knew he should try and keep himself awake, and I suppose the package of coffee was still where he had left it on arriving—it was spilt mostly just around the cupboard on the left inside the kitchen door according to your chaps. He wasn't capable of making it, of course . . .'

'No,' said the Marshal quietly, 'but what an effort he was making to stay alive.'

'Perhaps. But at that point, anyway, he gave in, sat down at the kitchen table and fell asleep among the remains of his dinner. Your people brought me samples of the blood that was under the table and the traces of vomit where his head had lain. The next thing we know is that he wakes up—this would be about an hour before you found him next day—having slept off most of the barbiturate, but rather weak, he's lost quite a lot of blood, goes to the sink—maybe he still feels sick—and finds in the sink the coffee-pot with the remains of the Viennese coffee in it. It's nasty and it's cold and there isn't much of it, but he has to wake himself up enough to get help. He drinks it and it kills him. The last straw. His heart gives out."

'Would he have noticed how nasty it tasted, not then perhaps, but the first time?'

'Have you ever tasted Viennese coffee, so called? I can't believe the Viennese would drink it; it's flavoured strongly with figs.'

The Marshal grimaced.

'Quite. And this was a very thick, strong brew, lightly sugared in the pot, not in the cup—he added more sugar in the cup. Remember he was already upset, even the first time, and not very likely to take much notice—but I bet he didn't care for it, all the same.'

'Then why should he . . .'

'Why does anybody eat or drink something they find unpleasant, rather than spit the stuff out?'

'I suppose —' the Marshal pondered a while—'out of politeness.'

'Correct. Do you think he had somebody with him?'

'Why do you ask?'

'Well, I know only one person ate and drank, but it's odd that no further trace of that coffee was found, not even a container for it, and the police lab found a hair on his lapel. Woman's. Been tinted and waved.'

'You don't think it could have been his wife's?'

'I know it wasn't. I've seen her photograph. She's a natural blonde, almost white. Doesn't mean much, of course; he's just as likely to have picked it up in the train. I just thought that if there was a woman involved . . .'

'There may have been,' the Marshal said cautiously, in case any of this should get back. 'The old lady next door thought she heard a quarrel and a woman leaving, but she didn't see anything . . . and she's ninety-one . . . it's all very vague and nobody wants to cause his wife any more grief if it's not absolutely necessary.'

'You needn't worry about that—at least, I shouldn't have thought so. I said that the hair was tinted and waved, but these vanities apart, it was a grey hair.'

'It was?'

'Certainly. I don't know if it's any help.'

'It may be.'

'Of course, your own lab can give you more details, if you go round to them.'

A look of puzzlement was beginning to form on the Professor's face. The Marshal quickly distracted him.

'Perhaps, if this woman exists, she was responsible for the strange coffee . . .'

'And for the barbiturate in it—well, it's only a hypothesis, but fascinating, all the same, fascinating.'

'A hypothesis? You mean you personally don't think . . . ?'

'Exactly, my dear Marshal, I don't think, I only look, and look hard! It's up to you people to do the interpreting. The fact is that people do behave oddly, and it isn't always possible to follow their train of thought when they're under stress. Our Dutchman was under stress, remember that—all those cigarettes. He was apprehensive; maybe something went very wrong with him. I can only tell you what happened, not why, or even how. For all you or I know he may well have taken the stuff deliberately, got in a panic when the vomiting brought him to, fallen asleep, and then got up the courage to take another dose in the morning.'

'He would dissolve it himself?'

The Professor shrugged. 'Some people hate taking tablets.'

'And where would he get it, if he didn't normally . . . ?'

'Has anybody checked?'

'I don't know . . .'

'I should have thought somebody ought to, but that's your department. Even if you don't find out, though, what does that prove?'

'Nothing.'

'You don't think it was suicide, I gather?'

'No, I don't.'

'Well, to tell you the truth, neither do I. But we can only go on the facts, and the trouble is, Marshal, that, strictly speaking, we only have two facts: one, the rather dubious one of a hair that could have come from any-where, unless you find a suspect; the other, the rather more intriguing one of the two aspirins—like sprinkling yourself with a glass of water before throwing yourself in the river, what?'

They were nearing the exit again. The Professor stopped talking suddenly and flushed.

'Pardon me. I've just realized how long I've kept you talking, and you were saying you had to go round to the police labs . . . I'm afraid they'll have gone home.'

'Wasn't urgent,' mumbled the Marshal.

'I do beg your pardon. I tend to go on a bit once I get going. The clockwork Professor, my daughter calls me. Well, I'll let you get on.'

After this unwonted confidence, the Professor turned

and started off down the corridor. The Marshal was too embarrassed to stop him but the porter, without even looking over his newspaper, called out, as if automatically:

'Professor!'

'Yes, what is it?'

'You were going home.'

The Marshal got out first and slipped into his car, pretending not to notice.

'Cause of death, heart failure,' he muttered to himself as he drove back towards the city centre. In the dusky streets, lamps were lit outside restaurants where tables were set out among potted shrubs. Waiters were squeezing between them with plates held high above their heads, and woodsmoke drifted on the warm air, carrying the smell of grilled steak. Lamps were lit, too, along the river, where sky and water were fused in the same midnight blue and turquoise, and bats wheeled about under the shadow of the Santa Trinita bridge.

'Cause of death, heart failure . . .'

The Santa Trinita bridge is one way, but the Marshal drove along to it and stopped.

'I'll just have a word with that young lady on the corner . . .'

He didn't get out of the car, just opened the door and called:

'Franca! Oh!'

She came towards him, blowing clouds of smoke like a peroxided dragon. Her fixed smile faded when she saw who it was.

'What's up?'

'Nothing's up. I want some information.'

'Now then, what do I know . . . ?'

The Marshal was sitting in the kitchen in his old slacks and vest. It had been after ten when he got home and now it was almost midnight. He had cleared the formica table after eating bread and cheese, fetched in a sheet of foolscap and a pencil from the office, and sat down, frowning. He hadn't written anything on the paper in over an hour.

It reminded him of summer nights when he was a schoolboy. It must have been June he was thinking of because there were so many fireflies and because he was doing homework, which meant school hadn't finished. His mother used to clear the big kitchen table for him after his sister had gone to bed. He could remember very clearly the rough patch on the straw-bottomed chair that always left a red pattern on the backs of his legs, and the voice of his father and the other men coming from beyond the small, barred window, still unshuttered though it was already dark and the green fireflies winking. He would sit with his stockinged feet on the lower bar of the chair, always keeping his head down a little to look as though he were concentrating on the long piece of poetry he had been set to learn by heart. His mother would punctuate her brisk tidying and shoe-cleaning, saying 'That's right, you study; you get nowhere these days without studying. Your cousin Carmelo always studied.' Carmelo had been accepted into a seminary, his future was secure. 'You keep on studying, you don't want to spend your life slaving on the land like your father.'

Little did she know that all the time his big eyes were following her every movement between the stove, the sink and the storeroom, while his ears strained to catch every word of the conversation of the men who sat on the wall outside, gossiping and smoking under the stars. They were too far from the village to go to the café.

And each time his mother opened the storeroom door, he waited for the faint whiff of greek hay, mixed with the musty smell of the rabbits huddled in their cages.

Looking back on it now, he saw his father as having

been perfectly contented until the day they moved to the village after his retirement. After that he was disorientated and he soon fell sick and died. Now it was his mother, after having agitated so long for the move, who couldn't remember where she was, and whined like a small child to be taken home.

The fact remained that in those long-ago days he had never got much homework done, and he wasn't getting much done now. The lined paper was still empty.

The rhythmic sawing of the cicadas in the Boboli Gardens behind the palace was probably contributing to his fit of nostalgia for the country. But there was nobody out there gossiping under the stars. The garden gates were locked at sunset; this was Florence. The Marshal got up to close the inner shutters and then sat down determinedly.

'What do I know?' he asked himself again. 'I know that the Dutchman came down from Holland on the train—the Professor let that slip, so I suppose they must have found his ticket on him. He bought some food . . . did he go anywhere else before the flat? I need a train timetable . . . I need to see that ticket. If I'd any concrete evidence to offer I could ring the Lieutenant and he'd tell me . . . but I haven't.

'Anyway, if by any chance he picked a woman up on his way from the station, Franca will let me know tomorrow. Myself, I doubt it. So, he goes to the flat and eats alone. There was only one plate, I remember that. Then he has coffee. The woman must have been with him then . . . about eight, according to Signora Giusti. Did she make the coffee while he was still eating, I wonder? *It wasn't her* . . . Well, what if he was mistaken, or didn't want to believe it? That's not the same as lying. The woman goes away after a quarrel—what about? Don't know. Maybe he falls asleep. At any rate, before too long he starts vomiting, loses consciousness and then wakes up choking, scrabbles through the medicine cabinet—no, I forgot, he took some aspirin . . . with the coffee, I suppose, and he'd been smoking all the time . . . and yet, he did eat, after all, so even if he was anxious he couldn't have been exactly panic-stricken, or expecting to meet a dangerous enemy. Expecting someone, though . . .

'After cutting himself and trying to stop the bleeding, he goes to the kitchen and messes with coffee, can't cope, falls asleep . . . Next day he wakes, makes for the sink, maybe to vomit, finds the remains of the other coffee and drinks it . . . flavoured with figs, what an idea! Then where does he go? To the bedroom . . . the other rooms seemed untouched, and he was bleeding, would have bled on all those white dustsheets . . . to the bedroom, then. Why? To go to bed? No, he was trying to keep awake. Why, then? He had keys in his hand, but I heard one of the Lieutenant's men saying they weren't the keys of that flat. They could have been the keys of his house in Amsterdam, but what would he want with those?

'There must have been a third set then . . . *He always left me his keys so that . . .*

'The keys to Signora Giusti's flat! She has his keys, so why not? It was the obvious place to go for help but he probably had no clear idea of what time it was and he knew that unless the social worker had been, she wouldn't be able to get out of bed and let him in. If they turned out to be Signora Giusti's keys and he had been going for help, surely that proved that he didn't want to die?'

It didn't, of course, prove that he hadn't wanted to die the night before. People who commit suicide with sleeping pills expect to die quietly in their sleep, not to go through what he'd gone through.

Even so, the Marshal wrote something on the sheet of foolscap: the word 'keys'. He drew a circle round it and looked at it.

My dear Marshal . . . the fact is that people do behave

oddly and it isn't always possible . . .

It didn't prove anything, anything at all. Even though he was alone in his own kitchen, the Marshal blushed with shame and embarrassment. If a man like the Professor, an educated man, practically a genius, who could reconstruct a man's life from a few marks, was unwilling to commit himself about whether it was suicide, who was he to insist . . .

A whole army of competent, educated people rose up in the Marshal's imagination . . . the Lieutenant, young, yes, but he had studied at the *Liceo*, had done his officer training and knew foreign languages, he could telephone to Amsterdam if he needed to; he had men at his disposal for checking every detail, not to mention computers. He could talk to the Substitute Prosecutor or Professor Forli as one educated man to another. He didn't sit at the kitchen table with a bit of paper and a pencil, after bumbling around the city all day in a Fiat so small you could hardly get in it and a door that shut only if you banged it three or four times.

The word 'keys' stared up at him mockingly. Surely, the first thing you were supposed to find was a motive, or something like that? And how could he find out whether anyone benefited from the Dutchman's death? He couldn't. He had no right to. The Lieutenant was an officer, while he . . . he was just a guard, he had no business . . .

Why had the Dutchman come to Florence in the first place? A business trip . . . to see whom?

There he went again! And it was none of his business. He wasn't competent . . .

A fly lit on the formica table and started to feed on a crumb that the Marshal's hurried wiping had left behind. Squalid. His glass and plate were still in the sink, dirty. Slapping heavily but uselessly at the fly in his distress, he got up and began rinsing his crockery. Then he wiped the table again, excessively. If his wife were here at least there wouldn't be this to upset him on top of everything else . . . he hated squalor; it stopped him from thinking in peace.

If you could call it thinking . . .

The sheet of paper lay there with 'keys' and the pointless ring round it that tried to give the word more importance than it had.

'You're ignorant, that's what. Ignorant . . .'

He tossed the paper into the rubbish bin, switched out the light and went through the living-room and out to the office to switch the phone through to his bedroom. Automatically, he flicked on the close-circuit television for a moment to check the entrance. A laurel hedge and a stretch of gravel, pale in the moonlight . . . the back fenders of his little car, the van and the jeep. He switched off. There was no sound from upstairs; Gino's radio had been switched off an hour ago. They must all be asleep. Before turning out the light he noticed a little stack of matchboxes and a pile of loose change next to the telephone. It took him a few moments to register what they meant, then he picked them up and switched out the light.

'Ignorant,' he repeated on his way to the bedroom, thinking of the humble Gino who took pleasure in doing small things for other people, readily admitting that he had no brains. He did nothing but good in the world whereas somebody as presumptuous as . . .

You know, murderers don't go round attacking people with sleeping pills . . .

The Lieutenant could have given him a rocket for his cheek, and yet he didn't. He had been quite kind. Self-controlled. An officer and an educated man.

'She was right, was my mother,' he told himself as he cleaned his teeth, scowling at himself. 'She was absolutely right . . .'

In bed, he lay a moment looking at the photograph of

two plump little boys that stood on the chest of drawers opposite, before switching out the light.

'The thing is,' he remarked to his absent wife as he turned over and sank into the pillows, 'I feel as if I would have liked him. He was well off and yet he still worked with his hands . . . a craftsman . . . that's what I would have liked to be if I'd had any talent for it . . . and he didn't forget the old lady who'd looked after him when his mother died. There aren't many like that, these days. And yet, I really don't know anything about him, at all . . .'

CHAPTER 5

'So you thought you'd ask me—the same as your friend who came yesterday. You thought I was the one who knew him better than anyone, and it's true that I do. He was born in this building, and for a few years after his mother died I was the only mother he had, his *mammina*.'

'Somebody . . . somebody was here yesterday?'

'You know as well as I do. The officer you sent for that day. He came back here yesterday, asking questions. Just before lunch it was . . .'

So the Marshal had made some impression on the young Lieutenant, after all. Though perhaps he had been of the same opinion all along, and had only wanted encouragement. Signora Giusti was chuckling wickedly among her cushions.

'I don't mind saying there are things I'd tell you that I wouldn't tell a young whippersnapper like that—I don't mean him any ill, but fancy coming to see an old lady like me empty-handed.'

The Marshal's offering, a little cardboard tray of profiteroles with three colours of icing, lay open on the occasional table between them, its gold and white paper wrapping and yellow ribbons strewn over the telephone.

'I've always had a sweet tooth, I'll admit . . .'

The tiny, soft-boned hand reached out to the tray. 'And these days I can manage to eat so few things—look! Look at that! It's the same every morning.'

A rug was being shaken from the window below. Signora Giusti leaned forward until her forehead was touching the glass, and counted the billows of dust that floated out over the gloomy courtyard.

'Three, four, five, six! And she calls that clean! I'd have fired her the first day but that old witch downstairs has money to burn. She's only seventy, you know, but she claims to have a bad leg that stops her ever coming up here to see me. Does she think I don't see her from my bedroom window, hobbling up Via Romana? And do you know where she's going? The cinema, that's where! But her leg's too bad for her to come up two flights of stairs and spend an hour with me—so how is it she can manage to go up and down the six flights to her own flat? Who does she think she is, that's what I'd like to know! Does she think that when my husband was alive I'd have even thought of inviting a woman like her into my home? I've told her so, too. Oh, if you'd seen my drawing-room then . . . and now it's empty . . . even the carpets have gone, and they were Persian and good ones, too. Who does she think she is, just because she can afford a cleaner for two hours a day—and one who doesn't even clean properly—not that those rugs are worth anything, you can see that from here. Well, she needn't think I want her. I was doing her a favour, asking her up here, but people don't realize, they don't realize . . .'

She cupped her hands under her sunken face and cast about her in despair at the pathetic remains of her prosperous, bourgeois world; the photographs in their silver frames, the sad decorations round the picture of the

Pope, the rickety kitchen table with its checkered oilcloth cover.

'I'm too old, too old,' she wailed. 'I ought to be dead . . . this is what it comes to in the end, if you outlive your time.'

'Now, now, Signora. Now, now . . .'

'You don't know. You can't imagine what it comes down to. I'm nobody. I'm just an old woman, any old woman. I've no social position, no place in the world, no personality. There's nothing left of me. There's nobody left who knew me when . . . There's nothing to be said about me except that I'm ninety-one.'

'It's not true that you've no personality,' said the Marshal truthfully, for her viciousness was known and sometimes even feared. But then, he realized, that was probably deliberate, her bid to be recognized as a person instead of patronized as just another 'old dear'.

She was weeping now. The handkerchief she pulled from her pocket was an old lace-edged one, badly torn and stained but with her initial still visible on it. He pushed the cakes towards her, not knowing what else to do.

'I don't like the chocolate ones,' she snapped.

'Then here—' he turned the tray round—'there's a vanilla one left.'

She sniffed and took it, pushing it down between sobs.

'What sort of things did you not want to tell the officer yesterday?'

'Just little things, family things. Things that were told me in confidence, you understand. A youngster like that . . . well, you're a family man, I can tell. A good family man, not the sort to dump his old mother in a hospital, the way they do nowadays—is your mother still alive?'

'Yes, yes, she's still alive,' murmured the Marshal, 'although she's in very bad health . . .'

'But you're not the sort to dump her in a hospital and go off on your holidays?'

Her wily old eyes, glittering with tears, were piercing right through to his conscience. It was uncanny the way some women knew by instinct where to prod so as to cause the most pain, even when they knew nothing at all about a person.

'No, of course I wouldn't . . .'

That sort of instinct was perhaps what made a good detective, an instinct for which questions to ask of a suspect, where to put the pressure. But in any case, he didn't have a suspect. He didn't have the instinct, either; but Signora Giusti did, and she knew more than anyone about the Dutchman and his family. If he could only keep her to the subject! But no, she was off again on her reminiscences.

'I suppose you've got children. I never had any. How she gloated over that! It was the one thing that induced her to speak to me at last. The husband was no better—I suppose he was jealous because we were rather well-to-do, and that bitch of a sister of mine wouldn't be likely to let him forget it. He was a railway clerk, nothing more. Oh, he became some sort of head of department in the end, but they always had to be careful about money, while of course my husband was an engineer and was very highly thought of, as well as highly paid. There was money in the family, too, naturally; I wouldn't have had him otherwise. I could take my pick, I can tell you, with my looks. We inherited all our silver, apart from wedding presents, it had been in his family for years. And now it's almost all gone . . . If I'd had children who could have supported me . . . I'll never forget the baptism party, and that pompous little idiot of a husband of hers in his stiff collar that looked as if it was going to choke him . . .

' "We're grateful to Our Lord, Maria Grazia, that he's sent us a son to comfort us in our old age." What a fool! And she just stood there simpering with the child in her arms, not troubling to hide her triumph. The son was killed during a bombing raid when he was in Rome during the last war, anyway . . .

'We left their wretched baptism party as soon as we decently could, but although you could say the big quarrel ended that day, we never became close.'

'What started the quarrel?' asked the Marshal, not at all sure who she was talking about but hoping somehow to find an opening.

'Jealousy. They say money's responsible for most of the trouble in the world, but if that's true then jealousy comes a close second, and jealousy between sisters is the most vicious of all, and the most unreasonable. After all, I couldn't help having the looks I was born with. Oh, but I was beautiful!'

She glanced across, bright-eyed, at the photograph of herself, as though it were of someone else.

'And the offers I had! Do you know I'd received five proposals of marriage by the time I was seventeen? What do you think I should have done? Refused the man I wanted to marry just because my sister, who was three years older, couldn't get herself a husband at any price? Was my life to be ruined, I ask you? It wasn't that she was ugly, you know, but she had a sour temperament, no gaiety in her. Eventually she took to being pious, never away from church and forever doing good works. Then she takes the first man who offers himself. He looked like a draper! I ask you! I couldn't resist calling him her draper when I went home to visit — never directly, you know, just a little teasing. I'd ask her how he was and then bring the conversation round to the new season's silks, asking her advice and then asking her what *he* thought and whether she couldn't get something for me at a discount!'

She went off into peals of laughter, rattling among her cushions, and the Marshal wondered how the unfortunate sister had kept from strangling her. On and on she went, and each time he tried to bring up the Dutchman, she

would make some tantalizing remark and then plunge
into more unpleasant reminiscences. He began to wonder
how the Lieutenant had fared yesterday. It seemed
unlikely that he had got anything out of her, but the
Marshal was willing to bet that she hadn't dared play with
an officer the way she was playing with him now.

There seemed little doubt that she was doing it quite
deliberately, for she was unquestionably sound of mind
and not rambling inadvertently. It could be, of course, he
thought more charitably, that she was just trying to spin
out his visit as much as possible. The social worker had
been leaving when the Marshal arrived, having left a cold
lunch prepared. It was only ten o'clock now, and a day of
sitting alone, looking out at the gloomy courtyard, was all
the old lady had to look forward to. If she had anything to
tell, she would make the most of it, spreading the information over as many visits as possible.

He had hoped, at first, that her distress at the death of
her beloved Toni would induce her to help him find out
what had happened, but now he was beginning to understand a little of what it meant to be ninety-one years old.
She had buried all the members of her own family, and
seen off all her friends and enemies one by one. She was
ready to die herself. For her, the division between the
living and the dead was not the same as for a young person; the dead who had been part of her own world and
who had known her in her hey-day were more alive for
her than the living generations for whom she didn't
count. It didn't distress her that the young Dutchman
should be dead so much as that, once again, she had been
left behind . . .

'It was the same thing there, you see, jealousy.'

'I'm sorry . . . ?'

'I thought you wanted to hear about Toni's family. You
said that's what you came for.'

She *was* teasing him, now he was sure. She had noticed

his gaze wandering and had immediately begun to talk about the Dutchman. She evidently intended to drift off again, now, but the Marshal suddenly leaned forward with his large hands on his knees and stared at her fixedly, saying very deliberately:

'Jealousy of whom?'

His sudden change of attitude disconcerted Signora Giusti, and she answered him obediently:

'I was talking about Toni's stepmother, Signora Wilkins, as she was before she was married to Goossens. All that trouble she had with her sister, her elder sister, there was a year between them, it was all jealousy and I told her so. It could have been my story over again, only with them it happened twice, in a manner of speaking. Not that Signora Wilkins took it the way I did; she wasn't one to tease or take advantage — oh, you needn't look surprised, I know my faults; I've always been selfish and I've always had a sharp tongue in my head, and I might as well admit it now that my life's over and it's too late to reform. But Signora Wilkins is a very different sort of person. She was good-looking in her younger days, but never played on it, if you know what I mean. She married first, just as I did, but she married a man who had virtually nothing except ideas and energy. I don't think her family was too pleased and the sister was downright scornful. Reading between the lines, I'd say that she was sweet on young Wilkins herself but she wasn't going to marry anybody without money and position, not she. Well, the wedding came off and I gather that the young fellow did all sorts of jobs before he got his idea.'

'What sort of idea?' Would they *ever* get to the Dutchman?

'I'm telling you, if you'll listen. It seems that in the northern part of England they make cloth, something like Prato, I imagine, an industrial area, cotton and so on. Well, like in Prato, the local people could buy cloth for almost nothing, buying straight from the factory, the end pieces and pieces with a tiny fault, whole bales sometimes. Anyway, Wilkins was up there travelling for a firm and he got this idea of buying up this stuff and taking it south to where they lived—don't ask me to pronounce it, I couldn't begin to try. He could sell it down there for twice what it cost him and it would still be a good bargain compared to shop prices—I used to laugh to myself when Signora Wilkins talked about it. After all, *she* really did marry a draper, didn't she, of a sort? That's why I've never mentioned to her about the jokes I used to make about my sister. It might have offended her . . .'

The Marshal pondered on the Englishwoman who had managed to bring out what good there was in Signora Giusti's selfish little heart. She must have been something special because nobody else seemed to escape that sharp tongue.

'And did he do well?'

'He did more than well, he made a fortune. It was an awful risk at first, because of course he had to give up his job. She had savings but not much; they only had a few months in which to make a go of it. He started off by carting the stuff down on the train in suitcases, and she would go with him and help him—and she hadn't been brought up to a life like that, I can tell you; I think her father was a solicitor. They travelled to the north and back three times a week and then he stood in the market-place with his suitcases open on the floor; they didn't even have a stall. But people fought to get at it, she used to tell me, fought to get at it! It was all fine quality stuff, you see, usually with some tiny, almost invisible fault running through it. There was brocaded upholstery, sheeting, towelling, everything . . .

'Before long they got a stall and then a little van. They never had children but as soon as they were comfortably off he insisted that she stay at home. She was more sorry than glad because those first few hectic years when they were always exhausted and often hadn't enough to eat were happy ones. Even so, she agreed to stay at home and they soon had such a large house that she was kept busy. The business got bigger and bigger and he took on some assistants so that he could cover more than one market at a time. But he still did all the buying himself; he had no desire to be just a businessman who left all the active work to others.'

The Marshal was beginning to understand. Apart from the difference in trade, it could have been the Dutchman. Did the Dutchman take after his father? If so, he could understand why the father and Signora Wilkins had married. But that must have been much later . . .

'What happened to him, then, this Signor Wilkins?'

'He died rather suddenly. She was heartbroken, but they'd had a good many happy years together by then. They used to travel a lot, she loved to tell me about that. She'd seen the world—even sailed up the Congo once in a cargo boat, can you imagine? It wouldn't suit me, all those black men, and it couldn't have been very clean, but her eyes used to light up when she talked about it. Oh, the hours we spent chatting together. If only she'd stayed here . . .

'They loved Italy more than any other place; they had their first real holiday here, and after that, wherever else they went they always spent some time here every year. They saw more of this country than you or I are ever likely to. They used to drive round, stopping wherever suited them. They learned the language, too, and read a lot—nothing studious, you know, but stories and histories of the places they visited. They were never happier, she always says, than when they were here, as is only natural. I've never been to England myself but they say the weather's very grey and there's no wine grown. I'm not a great wine-drinker myself and never have been, but imagine there not being any . . . it's not civilized . . .'

'No, no,' murmured the Marshal, trying to imagine a grey world without vines but not succeeding. It seemed to him unlikely.

'Anyway, when Wilkins died of a stroke, she came and settled over here. They'd often talked about it as something they might do when he retired.'

'She must have been a very courageous woman, to set out on her own and in such sad circumstances.'

'Of course she was courageous! She'd had the guts to marry a man with nothing, against her family's wishes, and to work like a slave with him when she hadn't been brought up to it. Of course she was courageous — not like some I could mention who—'

'And the sister,' interrupted the Marshal firmly, 'did she marry, as yours eventually did?'

'Ah! She got what she deserved — not that she thought so. She married for money, a man a lot older than herself. She was even barefaced enough to say to Signora Wilkins that she fully expected him to die before too long and leave her comfortably off! After that she thought she'd find somebody she liked better! But all her grasping ways did her no good at all; her husband fell ill but he didn't die, not for eleven years! It turned out he was a diabetic but nobody had known, until one day he crushed his finger in a door. He had it dressed but it didn't heal. Instead, it began to stink — gangrene! Can you imagine? He lost part of the finger and started treatment for diabetes, but it got steadily worse. By the end he'd lost a leg and his eyesight was failing rapidly. So, instead of quickly inheriting his money, she had to nurse him. It doesn't bear thinking about, the sort of life she led him once she found out that there wasn't any money either! It seems he'd fancied himself as a speculator, and once he was bedridden and she took over his affairs she found that he had nothing but a lot of worthless shares. She had no choice but to write to her sister, who was settled out here by then, and ask her for money. I gather they were even in danger of being evicted, of having their mortgage foreclosed. At any rate, Signora Wilkins gave her money, I don't know how much, and the use of her house in England. She told me she was glad to have somebody living in it; that it was immoral to leave it standing empty and she couldn't bear to think of selling. But I warned her, I said, you'll have nothing but trouble from that one. I'd seen it all before. She's jealous of you, I told her— Goossens was on the scene by then, so that was another reason for jealousy. But poor Signora Wilkins, she wouldn't have it. She wouldn't see wrong in her own sister—I sometimes think it was because there was no evil in herself that she couldn't recognize it in others. It doesn't do to be that innocent in this world. But then, she was happy herself and wouldn't wish anybody ill.'

'Where did she meet Goossens?'

'Here in this house. She took the flat below—not the one on the right where that old witch is, the one on the left where the young couple live now. Goossens and little Toni were up here across the way, as you've seen. His first wife was Italian but she died of cancer, poor creature, when the child was only ten. Toni, I ought to call him Ton but I never do, spent a lot of his time here with me while his father was downstairs in the workshop.'

'So that was his place, in those days?'

'Certainly it was. He started it. He was from Amsterdam and he had a business there, but he'd always come to Florence, mostly to buy designs. He was a good craftsman and said so, but he was no artist, and Italian design, he used to tell me, is famous the world over. He was a cutter, himself, and would bring stones to the jewellers down here and buy designs. When he met and married his Italian wife they lived in Amsterdam for a while but it seems she never settled. She'd never been abroad before and spoke no language but Italian . . . and then the cold . . . So, eventually, he set up a workshop downstairs and he bought this flat up here.'

'Was his wife in the jewellery business, too?'

'She was a designer. He'd always admired and bought her work—but don't think it was a marriage of convenience because he wasn't that sort. He grieved for years when she died. It was a sad household for that little boy. It was just after she died that he was taken badly with rheumatic fever.'

'At least he had his *mammina*.'

'I did what I could, but I wasn't young, you know, even then. Think about it: when Toni's mother died he was ten and I would be sixty-one and already widowed. I couldn't be running about. Goossens still travelled a lot between here and Amsterdam. He'd put a manager in the workshop up there so as not to have to leave the child too often, but he was still taking up designs and bringing down stones to cut here. I looked after the child, but he would never sleep here. I always went over there . . . even when he had the fever . . . It often crossed my mind that he couldn't bear to leave the house empty . . . as if he thought his mother might one day come back. It's hard to believe in forever at that age. Anyway, you see why I've always had their keys . . .'

'And did you,' asked the Marshal, remembering the ringed word on a sheet of foolscap, 'give him—the son, I mean—your keys, for this flat?'

'Of course. He still has them . . . had them . . . poor Toni . . . why didn't he come to me? I don't understand it at all.'

'I believe he was trying to. He had your keys in his hand, if I'm not mistaken, when I found him. Do you mind if I get a glass of water?'

She was silent until he sat down again, shedding a few tears that, this time, were not tears of self-pity. She was absorbed in her memories and didn't notice when the window below opened again for a duster to be shaken out into the shady courtyard.

'And so,' prompted the Marshal, 'then he met Signora Wilkins . . .'

'Right here in this flat. She'd soon got into the way of popping up to see if I needed anything. I don't think she let a day pass without calling in on me for at least a moment. She had no need to work, of course, but she couldn't bear to be idle. One day she came up and asked me what I thought of the idea of giving English lessons to the local children. She wanted to do it without taking payment but I persuaded her against that; people would have thought it peculiar, and if it comes to that, there are always those who don't pay up, she needn't have worried. It was the company she wanted, that and the idea of doing something useful for somebody. Her first pupil was young Toni. Goossens was delighted. He didn't expect the child to learn Dutch, but it seems that most Dutch people speak English, and Toni would have to take over the business some day and deal with Amsterdam. There were other pupils too, of course, but anyway, Toni was the first, and that's how she and Goossens met.'

'And then she became your next-door neighbour?'

'Not right away. I'll tell you something that I wouldn't tell anybody else: they were married more or less in secret, and she kept her flat downstairs for a year after that . . .'

The Marshal shifted uncomfortably on his hard chair which was a good deal too small for him; his back was beginning to ache. Signora Giusti, however, was showing no sign of flagging. sometimes leaning forward to rattle her tiny hands at him, sometimes tossing herself back into her cushions and chattering reminiscently at the ceiling.

'It was the child, you see. He was a quiet, sturdy boy but very sensitive. He had his father's heavy build but his mother's big dark eyes and artistic temperament. As pupil and teacher the two got on like a house on fire, but once he saw what was developing between her and his father he clammed up. It was a very tricky time for all three of them, and she sometimes came to me in tears. She'd never had a child of her own but she'd always wanted one and her heart went out to Toni. She had all the patience in the world with him, but there wasn't a scrap of response—not that he ever said a wrong word, you understand, he was always polite, always well-behaved. In the end, he began to behave in the same way to his father. They were in despair, the two of them. I often wondered if he just felt they wouldn't want him around and he was trying to show his independence. He must have thought a lot about his mother during that time, too. Who knows? He might have been fighting against Signora Wilkins because it seemed like a betrayal. There's no knowing what goes on in a child's mind.'

'How old was he then?'

'He'd be about fourteen because that summer he finished Middle School and started in the workshop with his father. There was a change in him right away. I suppose he must have felt he had a place in his father's world, after all. He worked like a little slave, I can see him now, filing away hour after hour at his bench, so desperately anxious to do everything just right. If he made the slightest mistake his eyes would fill up and his face redden.

'Then, one day, he broke a small file. I don't know how. Instead of telling anybody, he hid it. It was a week before anybody noticed—there were three other crafts-men in the studio and they all tended to stick to their own set of tools—and Toni got paler and more worried every day; nobody knew why, of course. In the end, he needed the file for some small job he'd been asked to do. He was terrified. His father was a stolid, even-tempered man and had never struck the boy in his life; nevertheless, he was a craftsman, and very strict about the way the studio was run. Looking after the tools was the first thing Toni had had to learn. Well, he came up here to me and he broke his heart. It seems ridiculous, looking back on it, especially as it turned out the file had been an old, slightly damaged one that they'd given him to practise with—though, of course, he didn't know that. I think he would have run away from home, you know, over a little thing like that, if I hadn't been here.'

'It happens. I've known children run away for less, and in less strained circumstances.'

'Well, luckily he had his *mammina* to run to instead. I was close to him but not involved, if you see what I mean, and then, I'd known his mother and I think that counted for a lot. I can see him now; he sat at that table there and broke his heart, great big sobs without a tear. I've never seen a child cry like that . . . His nerves were shattered and there were great black rings under his eyes . . . crumpled up there with his head on the table . . .'

It was more real to her, that day in the distant past, than the scene in the bedroom two days ago. But the Marshal, looking at the oilcloth-covered table where the young boy in his apprentice's black smock had wept, was seeing the figure crumpled behind the door, a towel bound uselessly round one hand.

'They're the only people who mean anything to me. The people round her, like that witch downstairs . . .'

'What happened about the file?'

'Well, of course Toni was missed and his father came looking for him here. Funny, he was a big, clumsy sort of man, although he did such fine work. In a crisis like that he stood there with his big, clever hands all limp. You could see that every one of the boy's sobs went right through him, but he wasn't a demonstrative man and he didn't know what to do. In the end I poured out a drop of vinsanto for him to give the child—and he was so distracted he began to drink it himself! I had to push him towards the table. Toni took a sip or two and then started on about the wretched file, trying to apologize; then he flung himself at his father and started to cry real tears.

'That was the crisis over with. After that his work came on like nobody's business. He had his father's feeling for solid craftsmanship, but there was Italian blood in him, too. "He's an artist," his father would say to me, time and time again, "He's an artist. I can teach him craftsmanship, but he knows things I don't know . . ."

'Every spare minute Toni had, he would draw, designing every sort of gold work and settings for the jewels he saw his father cutting. There was a ring he designed that impressed his father so much that he decided they should make it together. It was in gold, and young Toni had never worked in gold—this was still his first year and he had only recently been given a small piece of silver to work on after having had only copper to learn on. Nevertheless, his father let him make part of the setting—but then, he was a very talented boy, there's no doubt about that, and gold is so much easier to work than harder metals, "like carving butter, *mammina*," he used to say to me, "just like carving butter!"

'It was a really special ring and it's hard to describe it . . .' She was turning her own hands over each other as if feeling for the shape of it in her memory.

'It had a double layer of gold, a plain, broad, flat band with a layer of filigree over it, slightly broader. It gave the effect of fine lace over smooth silk, if you can understand me, and the overlapping, lacy edge had the tiniest possible stones in the border—each stone different and rather odd in shape; a miniature lozenge-shaped pearl, a brilliant sapphire, hardly bigger than a full stop, a slightly larger ruby, and three diamonds, all small, set between the two layers of gold so that they were only just visible, peeping through the "lace".'

'Must have cost something . . .' said the Marshal thoughtfully.

'I should say it did . . . but perhaps not as much as you'd think; the stones were very small and not of great value, and it's the workmanship that's the biggest expense—that one piece took the two of them months to finish; they used to work on it together when the studio was closed in the evenings. They kept it a secret from everybody until it was finished, and those hours they spent together unbeknown to anyone must have put the boy right. It was just the sort of attention he needed, I suppose. Anyway, they finished it. It was a unique piece, unrepeatable because of the peculiarity of the little stones. Nevertheless, it brought them in thousands of pounds' worth of business—it was on show downstairs in the saleroom behind the studios for a time, and the original drawings for it are still there now, although the business has been taken over by Signor Beppe, as they call him, one of Goossens's craftsmen who's always worked there.'

Here was yet another area in which the Marshal felt conscious of his total ignorance. He knew no more about diamonds, cut or uncut, than an occasional glance into the jewellers' windows on the Ponte Vecchio could tell him. Would a ring like that eventually have such value that someone would kill to get it? Or had the Dutchman, when he came down to Florence on Sunday, been carrying diamonds, legally or illegally? This was an international trade about which he knew nothing; and these people, English and Dutch, who seemed to be at home anywhere in Europe, were beyond his understanding. His only contact with foreigners was when they lost their Instamatic cameras. The rest of his time was spent reporting stolen Fiat 500s that never got found because looking for them was like looking for a wisp of hay in a haystack. Or he spent it trudging round hotels routinely checking registers. For the second time, he felt seriously like giving the whole thing up. He felt he was chasing ghosts, and the only result was likely to be that he would make a great fool of himself. And yet, the Lieutenant had taken the trouble to come round here . . .

'You said,' he suddenly remembered, 'that the trouble with Signora Wilkins's sister happened "twice over", didn't you?'

'And so it did. When Goossens died, you see, he left everything to his wife, naturally, and so there was more fuel for the sister's jealousy—I always maintained that it was a mistake to have invited her to live out here.'

'She lived here? What was her financial position then? Had the diabetic husband died?'

'Oh yes, he died all right, and she was still penniless.'

'What about insurance?'

'I don't know, not for sure. But I do know she had nothing. Often, when there'd been a scene and the Signora would come round here in tears, I'd say she should throw her out, it was ridiculous to tolerate her nastiness, I said, after all you've done for her. But she always said she couldn't, that you couldn't put your own sister out on the street, that she had nothing. It wasn't strictly true, of course, because I do know that the allowance she'd paid her during the diabetic husband's illness went on being paid. She didn't want her sister to feel dependent, to have to ask for money when she wanted it. Imagine wasting such delicate feelings on somebody who'd strangle you for two pins! At any rate, I'm pretty sure that her going on with the allowance meant that there'd been no insurance. It was never mentioned openly, but Toni once let slip to me that there'd been talk of suicide, so maybe the insurance people had refused to pay up . . .

'Anyway out here she came, and the English house was let. "You'll rue the day," I told her, and I think she did, too, though she never said so in as many words. The more kindly and generous she was, the more it infuriated her sister who wanted to be respected and envied, not pitied. There were some shocking scenes, I could hear them from here. Then threats of suicide, then trips to the doctor's—that all had to be paid for—imaginary illnesses and more threats of suicide. But don't you believe it, was what I used to say. People like her make sure they don't damage themselves, only the people around them get hurt. She'll outlive both of us, I used to say . . . Well, I suppose I might have been wrong there, but even so . . .'

Even so, right in principle, the Marshal thought, though it seemed now as though Signora Giusti was all set to outlive her every acquaintance.

'What was it,' he said aloud, 'that you didn't like to tell the officer, yesterday?'

'I answered his questions, he can't say I didn't.'

'But some questions he didn't ask, is that it?'

'A youngster like that . . . he wouldn't understand the things that can go wrong in families. I doubt if he's even married.'

'Even so, he must be part of a family.'

'I hadn't thought of it like that.'

'What went wrong?'

'Well, I always said that nothing went right after old Goossens's death. There's always one person who holds everything together in a family, one person that everyone respects or at least that nobody wants to quarrel with, then when that person dies . . . Usually it's a woman but in this case it was old Goossens; he was quiet and solid, never quarrelsome . . .

'Toni always blamed the sister, though he admitted he had no concrete reason, but I still maintain that it was one of those things that happen once the central figure of the family dies, up to then all disagreements and the like are kept under control, but after that person dies, sooner or later they break out. If old Goossens had lived . . . well, he didn't, and whatever the reason was behind it — and I've never known — Signora Wilkins, Goossens I should say — and I'll not hear a word said against her, whatever you think . . . The fact is that she left this house on the day of the funeral and she's never been back here since. I don't know where she is to this day and neither does Toni. And it's been ten years, think of it! I wasn't at the funeral, I was already past being able to get about, and she never said a word to me before going out that day, not a word . . . She'd locked herself in alone with her grief for days.'

She sat back in her cushions and dabbed at her eyes.

'I was the one who had to let Toni know she'd gone off just like that. He was working in Amsterdam by then, you see; his father had sent him up there five years before to learn cutting, and to take over the Amsterdam end of the business. Toni had just met Wanda, the girl he married, and they were thinking of getting engaged, I remember . . .'

'Had there been a quarrel? Even if he was in Holland and his stepmother here, there could have been a disagreement, by phone or by letter. There could have been money troubles after the father's death, couldn't there? It's the sort of thing that breaks families up all the time.'

'No. All that was settled very fairly. They were both well provided for, and Toni swore to me that there hadn't been a quarrel, not one ill word.'

The Marshal mopped his brow with a large white handkerchief. He was feeling out of his depth again. There were two many ins and outs in this family and he wasn't at all sure that he was asking the right questions. He tried to introduce a note of common sense.

'Why didn't he just report her missing to the police? She might have had an accident, lost her memory, turned a bit strange . . .'

'No; she wasn't missing, not in that sense. Toni had a

letter from her solicitors in England saying she was breaking off all communications with him and that anything urgent could be dealt with through them. He telephoned them right away but he couldn't get anything out of them except that she'd settled in some other part of England and had been in touch with them by letter, instructing them to sell the house which up to then she'd only ever rented out. Toni would have gone after her, searched the whole country, but Wanda, his fiancée, wouldn't have it. You can't blame her, of course, because she'd never known her. All she knew was that she was Toni's stepmother and had behaved badly, going off like that and upsetting him. She's a gentle creature, but when it comes to defending her own . . . She felt it was just asking for more upset, going after her, and she put her foot down. Oh, but he took it all badly, did Toni . . .'

'But surely the girl was right. She was only his stepmother, after all, not his mother, and if she'd stated so clearly that she wanted no more to do with him . . .'

'You don't understand! You don't understand at all. Remember how, even when she and Goossens were married, she was too delicate to move into their flat because she wasn't sure how Toni would take it?' She waited almost a year, that's how much she thought of that child! Then came the ring. When it was finished Toni and his father presented it to her. It was Toni's own idea. It was like a second wedding, and she moved in that same week. Up to then, nobody but me had known they were married.

'Well, after that everything went well. She was like a young girl again once she had people to look after. She ran the house and helped with the business . . . and they travelled together, too. She used to say God had given her two whole lives, that she was living her youth all over again. And I'll tell you another thing: she loved Goossens and they were always happy together, but the greatest

thing of all, for her, was having Toni. All her life she'd
wanted a child, you see . . .

'Let me show you something . . .' She reached for her
walking chair but sank back again. 'In the table drawer,
get the photographs out . . . no, not the album, the two
that are framed . . . that's right . . . now see for yourself.'

They were enlarged colour snapshots, taken on
holiday. In one, the burly, grey-haired Goossens stood
with his arm around his small English wife. The sea was in
the background and a deep blue, clear sky; but there
must have been a breeze because the woman was holding
back her wavy hair which threatened to blow across her
face. In the second snap, which had obviously been taken
by Goossens, Toni, a strapping youth of about seventeen,
built like his father but with a more delicately modelled
face and merry dark eyes, was lifting his stepmother
bodily and threatening to toss her into the waves which
were lapping his feet. He was in swimming trunks but she
was wearing a white sundress with red spots on it. Both of
them were helpless with laughter, the sort of wholly
relaxed nonsensical gaiety peculiar to happy families.

The Marshal gazed at this photograph longer than was
necessary. He would soon be at the beach with his boys,
but by the time they got accustomed enough to each other
for that sort of laughter it would be time for him to leave
them.

'I put them in the drawer so as not to upset Toni when
he came. They used to be on the wall. I suppose I could
put them back now, or you could do it for me . . .'

The Marshal found the hooks where the pictures had
left patches on the wall and hung them up carefully.

'No, that one at the other side . . . that's how I had
them before . . . You can just see the ring, if you look
closely, but not enough to tell what it was like because her
hair's in the way. She never took it off.'

'I thought you said it was displayed in the saleroom?'

'It was, for a month after they gave it to her—she was so proud of the boy's design, you see, and wanted all the foreign buyers to see it; she often received them, that was how she helped with the business. She was never tired of boasting about Toni's work. Eventually, Goossens put the drawings up in the saleroom but they both insisted that she wear the ring. She never took it off again, though she sometimes worried about putting on weight and not being able to get it off to clean it—it was such a delicate thing, you see, not like a wedding-ring . . . oh dear, if only she were still here, I wouldn't be left alone, then, with nothing but my memories and an empty flat next door.'

'I'm surprised he hasn't sold it,' remarked the Marshal, thinking of the large number of homeless people in the city and a big place like that lying empty, to be used only for a few days a year.

'He can't. It was left to him in his father's will on the condition that his stepmother was free to live in it for the rest of her life. She's never been near it since the day she left but he couldn't sell it—not that he would have done. He always hoped she'd come one day.'

I wonder, thought the Marshal, if she did . . .

But looking again at the photographs, he refrained from wondering aloud. This was hardly the thin-lipped creature he had imagined when he was nodding off! Instead, he asked:

'Did you tell the officer, yesterday, about Toni's bringing stones down with him on these trips?'

'He already knew; perhaps Wanda had told him, but in any case Toni was a registered importer and exporter. He told me Wanda won't be coming down for the funeral, she's in a bad way.'

'He's to be buried here?' The Marshal was surprised.

'So it seems. I imagine it's the mother-in-law's decision, perhaps because Wanda's health won't stand any more upset so near the birth, but if you ask me, she's probably afraid of gossip with there being talk of suicide, although that young chap said that the death certificate would have "heart failure" on it. The mother-in-law's on her way down already . . . but I don't suppose she'll come and visit a useless old woman like me. Nobody else does . . .'

She got out her tattered lace handkerchief.

'Did you want to go to the funeral?'

'How can I go anywhere? I can't even get downstairs. I haven't been out of this house in ten years.'

It probably wasn't true, since she had talked of having been before to the convalescent home out in the hills. Even so . . .

'No, no,' she went on, sniffing. 'The next funeral I go to might as well be my own. I've seen enough people buried. I'd sooner have my memories. Nobody need come near me if they don't want to . . . I've no need of people like that selfish witch downstairs, and she needn't think I have . . . You'll have to let yourself out if you're going . . . I'll have a nap, I think.'

She was almost asleep, having suddenly run down like a clockwork doll, her tiny, sunken face lost among the cushions, and the Marshal tiptoed away along the passage to the front door.

On the next floor down a plump, elderly woman was watching for him in her doorway.

'How is she?'

'She's sleeping.' He hesitated, never one to preach. 'If you wouldn't mind going up some time . . .'

'I'll go up this evening at half past six, as usual. I don't like to think of her being alone in that last hour before she goes to bed . . . you understand what I mean. One of these nights she'll die in her sleep, more than likely. I make us both a hot drink and take it up. When I've seen her in bed I come down in time for the eight o'clock news which I don't like to miss— is something the matter?'

'No! No, I'm glad to hear . . .'

'I see. She's been telling you that nobody ever goes near her, I suppose. She tells everybody that, but the place is never empty, there's always somebody up there. She's none too pleased with me at the moment because I've a bad leg and once or twice I've had to go to evening surgery and miss our hour together. You mustn't believe the vicious lies she tells; it's her only pastime and she's too old to learn any other. Better that, anyway, than telling everybody about her bit of money. Has she . . . ?'

'Told me about her burial money? Yes.'

'I wish she wouldn't do that—oh, it's all right her telling you, but one of these days . . . I'll bet she was glad to see Signora Goossens back after all these years, at any rate; that should cheer her up. I've never heard her say a wrong word about *her*.'

'Signora Goossens?' Stupidly, he thought first of the Dutch mother-in-law who was coming down for the funeral, but of course she must mean . . .

'She's come back, did you say?'

'Wasn't she up there with you? I thought . . . well, I just caught sight of her going down past here when I opened the door, so then when you appeared . . . I can't think where else she'd have been unless perhaps to her old flat . . . I suppose there's no reason why not . . .'

'Did you speak to her?'

'No . . . no, I didn't, but then, I just glimpsed her hurrying down and naturally I thought she'd have been to see Signora Giusti—well, if I'd known you wanted to see her . . .'

But the Marshal was running heavily down the stairs, cap in hand, feeling for his dark glasses.

CHAPTER 6

The piazza was alive with people and sunshine, and the noise of the bellowing stallholders, gossiping women and barking dogs was overwhelming after the gloomy silence at the back of the old lady's flat. Only the dogs moved at speed, chasing each other round and round the fountain in the centre; everyone else was vociferous but heavy of limb in the overpowering heat of late morning. The Marshal's great eyes, protected behind the dark glasses, scanned the crowd under the trees hopelessly, for he didn't even know—apart from a twenty-year-old photograph—what the woman looked like.

'And if I did,' he muttered to himself grumpily, 'I'd never find her in this lot. She's probably half a mile away by now, in any case . . .'

He stood there uncertainly near a clothes stall, wondering what to do next. A short-legged, black and white mongrel trotted rapidly up to him, sniffed his shoes, then shot back into the dark doorway from which he had emerged. He belonged, presumably, to the flower-seller who had his kiosk-sized shop right beside the entrance to Signora Giusti's building. The Marshal turned back and looked in there, taking off his glasses to accommodate the gloom of the small, windowless rectangle. The smell of fresh vegetables was immediately masked by the scent of fresh flowers. A man in an artisan's black smock was sitting with his back to the narrow doorway, making the little posies surrounded by a coloured paper frill, some of which were hanging outside in the shade of a bit of striped awning. Only the back of the man's pale plump neck was visible.

'Make yourself at home,' he said, without looking up.

'I'm in a bit of a hurry,' said the Marshal, disconcerted not so much by this sudden remark as by the man's odd position, turned away as he was from the sunshine and the passers-by. 'I wondered if you'd noticed a woman come out from next door a few moments ago.'

The man rested his posy in the lap of his black smock and turned his closed and sunken eye-sockets in the direction of the Marshal, without a word.

'I'm sorry, I didn't realize . . .'

'A man in your job,' chuckled the blind man, 'might have thought to wonder why I don't sit in my doorway looking out. You'll find a little stool behind you, Marshal, if you want to sit down.'

He picked up the posy again and chose more flowers for it from a low table before him, his pale fingers caressing their heads to distinguish them.

'I did notice,' the Marshal defended himself, 'but I hadn't time to work out why. You know me, it seems?'

'You pass near here every day, except Thursday, on your rounds. You're very heavy and you walk slowly— looking about you, I imagine—and naturally I hear you answer when people call out "Good morning, Marshal." What else do you want to know? About the woman who seems to be trying to avoid you?'

There was no doubt that he intended to get as much mileage out of his story as Signora Giusti had out of hers, but the Marshal, much as he would have liked to allow the blind man his moment, was anxious to be off.

'Forgive an old man's vanity, Marshal. I can tell by your shuffling feet that you have to be off. A woman wearing medium high-heeled shoes came to the entrance of the building this morning and stopped dead outside. She hurried away past my doorway just as you arrived and went in, and then she came back again. She was walking up and down nervously outside here for a good hour, then, after hesitating for some time at the door, she suddenly went in and hurried up the stairs—she had a key, you see, so naturally I wondered what the problem was. Your being in there was the obvious answer. I also wondered who it was because it wasn't a tenant from that house, I know them all. Anyway, she came down in a great rush almost immediately, and you followed within a minute, so she must have spotted you or heard you starting down. Is she something to do with Signor Toni's death?'

'She may be. Do you know which way she went?'

'I wouldn't swear that she went away. I heard her crossing the cobbles towards the market stalls just over there, and then, of course, I lost track of her among the crowds. If you want to catch her you'd do well to hang about out of sight. After all, if she wanted to go in there . . . Forgive me, Marshal, I've no business to be telling you your job.'

He reached for a roll of pink crêpe paper and began to run it expertly through his fingers, stretching the edge into a frill.

'I'm glad of your help,' the Marshal said. 'I need all the help I can get.' His eyes were on the street outside. 'Tell me, do you remember a Signora Goossens, Signora Wilkins that was?'

'Certainly I remember her. She used to sit on that stool there and chat to me, especially in the early days when she knew nobody. I used to teach her Florentine proverbs and she collected them in a little notebook . . .' His pale, sightless face was lifted and he smiled a little at the memory. 'She loved flowers, you see; we had that in common. She knew all their names, too, and she liked to talk about her English garden. It was the one thing she really missed here. Later on, she was busier, after she was married, but she bought all her flowers from me. She never passed my door without calling out, "Good morning, Signor Botticelli, how are you?" And she often found time for a long chat when there wasn't a lot to do next door. Are you keeping an eye on the piazza?'

'Yes.'

'I thought you were. You know your job, I can tell that. You're a southerner, by your accent?'

'Yes.'

'I thought so. She was a good woman, Signora Wilkins, Goossens I should say . . .'

'And Signor Toni? Do you know much about him?'

'I know that tomorrow I'm to make a wreath for his funeral. It comes to us all in the end. If ever anyone upsets or tries to cheat me, that's what I say, I say, "Remember I make funeral wreaths, too." But I say it to myself. I'm making this one for Toni for the goldsmith next door. He could tell you more about Signor Toni; he owes him a lot. Maybe he owes him everything. He'll be at the funeral tomorrow, as will a good few other jewellers and goldsmiths in the city. If you go next door, ask for Signor Beppe, as they call him; he's the boss. You're not far from home, I suppose? From your Station, I mean?'

'No, Piazza Pitti.'

'Well and good. There'll be a storm before long. Perhaps you'll look in and say good morning some time on your rounds.'

'I will. And I'm grateful for your help.'

'Ask for Signor Beppe. I have a little bell here that I ring when I'm ready to close. The apprentice next door comes in and helps me pack up. It's not always the same time, you see, because I stop as soon as I've sold my day's flowers. I don't make a fortune, as you'll have gathered, but I'm not a burden on my daughter this way. I wouldn't want to sell lottery tickets like other people with my affliction do. I love flowers, you see. The scent and feel of them. I don't need to see them.'

'No.'

'Ask for Signor Beppe,' he repeated, feeling for a

bobbin of silver ribbon, 'and I'll be listening. If she comes back I'll ring my bell, in case you don't spot her. Come here, Fido, come on.'

He had slipped a biscuit from the pocket of his black smock, and the little black and white dog shot in, tail wagging, from the sunlit doorway.

Since the studio which had once belonged to the Dutchman had no licence to sell directly to the public, what had once been a shop window was covered over on the inside by large sheets of dusty white paper to conform with the law. There was a large tear in the paper, however, as was usual in such cases, a hole torn out at what would be the eye-level of a seated man. As he expected, the Marshal, when he had rung the ground-floor bell and been re-admitted to the building, opened the frosted glass door on the left and found an old man in shirtsleeves and a large canvas apron seated near the tear in the window-covering, polishing what looked like a stack of belt-buckles and glancing out now and then at the world going by outside.

'Good morning,' he said, looking up but still polishing away, 'What can I do for you?'

'I wanted a word with Signor Beppe, if he's here.'

'Certainly he's here. Go through that door there, straight through the workshop into the corridor beyond and take the first door on your left. That's the showroom where he receives buyers. He's got two Norwegians with him now, but if it's urgent . . .'

'It is. And if you don't mind, I'd rather speak to him here. I've got to keep an eye on the piazza.'

'In that case, you ought to have an assistant,' remarked the old man with brusque good sense. But he got to his feet.

The Marshal didn't deny it, but he sighed inwardly and said: 'I'll wait here.'

He stooped to peer through the torn hole in the paper,

only straightening up when he heard rapid footsteps behind him. Signor Beppe strode forward with his hand outstretched. He grasped the Marshal's large hand and wasted no time on preliminaries.

'Well? Have you some news for us about Toni?'

'Not exactly. You seem to know more than I do. The funeral's tomorrow, I hear?'

'That's right. You didn't know that? A young officer called yesterday to see Signora Giusti and I collared him. Somebody had to think about the funeral arrangements, after all. Wanda won't be coming down, that's his wife. My guess is she wanted to, but I gather the mother-in-law is a pretty forceful character. Not that Wanda hasn't inherited some of it—she knows her own mind—but in her condition she can hardly . . . Is something the matter?'

'No.' The Marshal straightened up. 'No . . . I just need to keep an eye on the piazza.'

'I see. Well, let's go to the front door, then, and talk there, save your back.'

'I'd rather be out of sight . . . I was surprised to hear he was to be buried here.'

'Nothing surprising about it. I know there's talk in the piazza about the family being afraid of some sort of scandal, but I can put you right on that score. There may be some truth in it, of course, given that there's been talk of suicide, which isn't a pleasant idea for a family to live with—but the fact is that he always intended to be buried here. It was in his will, to which I was a witness. He wanted to be buried with his father and mother, as is only natural. Some people round here called him the Dutchman, as they called his father, but Toni was born and bred here. He was one of us. He couldn't even speak Dutch, only enough to get by in business, and even for that he more often than not spoke English. See anybody?'

'No . . .'

'Am I allowed to ask who you're looking for?'

The Marshal hesitated. Signora Goossens seemed to be regarded as some sort of local saint. He wouldn't be too popular if he suggested he was keeping a watch on her, and he needed the information this man could give him. In the end he said:

'I'm watching to see if anyone comes in and goes upstairs who doesn't belong here.'

'Well, why didn't you say so? I can send my apprentice out to stand in the doorway, then if anyone goes in he can nip in here and tell you. Oh! Franco!'

The thin boy in a black smock, who appeared from some remote workroom, wiping his hands on a bit of rag, reminded the Marshal of that other morning and of the young Brother gently wiping the bloodstained oil from a dying man's palms.

'Go and stand at the front door,' instructed Signor Beppe, 'and if anybody at all, other than the tenants, tries to get in, run in here for the Marshal. Is the burner switched off?'

'Yes, I've finished . . . but I'm not sure if it's all right . . .'

'I'll come and look at it after. Out you go.'

The boy retreated.

'I'm teaching him annealing. Brings back the old days when Toni started. What his father didn't teach him, I taught him.'

'But you can't be much older, surely?'

'Six years. I was twenty when Toni started work.'

'You were here even then?'

'I've been here since I was twelve. I was old Goossens's first apprentice. Things aren't what they were in those days, of course. We made some jewellery then, and some really special stuff, too. I'm talking about for the Florentines, you understand. Nowadays they haven't the money. The nobility are poverty-stricken and the bourgeoisie, those that will spend, are more interested in how big a stone they can get for their money than in fine workmanship. A lot of the time we're being asked to repair or re-set pieces that people have inherited, and sometimes the piece isn't worth the real price of the work involved, but often it turns out to be a piece that's been made here and I do the work at a loss rather than turn old customers away.'

'Yet you seem to be doing well enough.' The Marshal's big eyes were taking in all the equipment in the room and glancing towards the corridor which he knew led to other studios and where he could hear people at work.

'Oh, I'm not saying we do badly, far from it. No, I'm talking about quality of work, not quantity. Nowadays, the good pieces we make are exported—I've got two Norwegian buyers here now and they'll take anything I can offer them, but this stuff—' he indicated the stack of oddly-shaped objects on the low table where the old man had sat polishing—'this is our bread and butter now, as far as Florence is concerned.'

'I can't quite make out what they are. Belt-buckles? No . . .'

Signor Beppe picked up one of the pieces and put it in the Marshal's hand.

'It's an initial . . . ?'

'It's an initial. And you'll recognize it when I tell you it will be attached to a very expensive leather bag or, if it's one of these smaller ones, to an equally expensive leather boot.'

The Marshal recognized it all right, but it wasn't a shop he was ever likely to set foot in unless one of its millionaire customers happened to get robbed as he was passing by.

'I couldn't begin to tell you how many of those things we make in a year—they export all over the world, apart from having branches in Paris and New York. Bread and butter, Marshal.' He flung the piece back on to the table. 'But not what a skilled goldsmith wants to spend his time doing. I've got my old dad to do the hours of hand polishing, which is something—he's not a skilled man himself but he likes to be useful, and at seventy-two . . . You're still nervous, I can see, but you needn't worry; the boy's reliable. Sit down on the stool, if you want to; my father's in the back looking after the customers.'

The Marshal perched himself on the edge of the low stool so that he could easily glance out into the piazza, scanning the crowded market as he talked.

'Not many people can afford an apprentice, these days,' he remarked. 'I was talking to a printer yesterday who said he couldn't even think of it . . .'

His voice sounded casual but his eyes were rolling from the window to Signor Beppe, round the room and back to the window, and his remark was anything but conversational.

'And neither could I, under normal circumstances. It's thanks to Toni that I can do that and other things . . .'

Maybe he owes him everything, the blind man had said.

'I bought this business from Toni when he decided to settle permanently in Amsterdam. In fact, I'm still buying it, and at a price so low and over a period so long . . . Well, I worked for old Goossens all my life and I taught Toni most of what he knew because his father was often travelling and I was set to help him, the senior craftsmen being too busy. Toni was never one to forget. His only condition in the sales contract was that I always trained an apprentice.'

'That must eat into your profits, even so. What happens now he's dead?'

'The payments will be made to his wife.'

'And the apprentice?'

'The arrangement remains the same. I don't keep the boy because I have to, Marshal. This business means a lot to me; I've worked here all my life. My own son's in the *Liceo Scientifico* and wants to study engineering, but continuity is what made this city what it is. If the crafts die out now for lack of apprentices . . .'

'What else was in the will?'

'Nothing of any interest: a few pieces of jewellery to his mother-in-law and the same to his stepmother who continues to have the right to live in the flat upstairs as his father would have wished. He had no other family—oh, and there's a small legacy for an old lady who lives upstairs.'

'Signora Giusti?'

'That's right.'

'Have you any idea why his stepmother left here so suddenly?'

'None, no . . .'

'You don't seem keen to speculate?'

'She was a good woman, and exceptionally good to Toni. He loved her very much.'

'Yet she left without a word—not even a word to you?'

'That's right. Immediately after the funeral. She didn't even take her belongings; it seems her clothes are still up there.'

It occurred to the Marshal to wonder if she had done the same after her first husband's death: walked away leaving everything behind her to start a new life in a different country. It wasn't impossible that she had married again. But it would be wiser not to say so just now. Instead he said:

'Toni must have been very upset?'

'He was.'

'But he never offered any explanation, mentioned any quarrel?'

'There was no quarrel. Toni wasn't even here when she left, he was in Amsterdam, and he knew of no explanation; he was as baffled as the rest of us. At first he telephoned and sent letter after letter through her solicitors, asking her just to see him and explain. Eventually his wife, Wanda, put her foot down. There was never any answer, anyway, so he more or less gave up . . . although recently . . .'

'Recently?'

'I'm thinking of the last time he was down here, which would be about four months ago. He seemed to think there was some hope of getting in touch with her.'

'He didn't say why?'

'No. Only that he felt she would have to come back now.'

'Without mentioning a reason?'

'No, just that he felt sure he would hear something, that she would have to come back now. I didn't press him because it was a subject that always upset him. He never really got over it.'

'Do you think it might have had anything to do with the baby they were expecting?'

'I suppose it could have been. After all, she was going to be a grandmother, so to speak, for the first time.'

'Nothing else in Toni's life had changed?'

'Not that I know of.'

'And how did he seem on that last visit?'

'Particularly cheerful. Mostly because of the baby—after eight years they'd almost given up hope.'

'Eight years? What was the problem?'

'That I couldn't tell you. I only know he was over the moon when the news was confirmed. He rang us up from Amsterdam.'

'Were you usually in touch with him in Amsterdam? I mean, he let you know when he was coming down? Signora Giusti said he sometimes telephoned her.'

'Yes, and me too, but not this time.'

'So apart from the phone call about the baby, you had no contact at all with him for the last four months?'

'I didn't say that. I said he hadn't let me know he was coming down. He wasn't due to come, not for another two months. Any business he did in Florence he did through this studio. He dealt with other jewellers besides me but we all met here; I arranged it as soon as he phoned. Between times you could say we were in touch because I sent him his mail. Some of it still arrived here, catalogues and bills mostly, and notices from the council, rates and such-like because he owned the property.'

'When did you send the last lot?'

'I think about three weeks ago. I don't send things one by one, I make up a package when there are a few — unless something looks urgent.'

'There could have been a letter from his step-mother in the last lot, then.'

'No, there couldn't. In the first place he'd sent her his address in Amsterdam after he married, through the solicitors, and in the second place, if she had written to him here I'd have noticed the letter.'

'You open them?'

'No, but as I said, I only make a point of sending on an individual letter if it looks important. I would certainly have noticed a personal letter with an English postmark, even telephoned him.'

'Had he ever asked you to do that?'

'Not in so many words but I knew how much it mattered to him.'

'Can you remember what was in the post you sent? Was there any personal mail at all?'

It needn't, after all, have been posted from England. If the woman was here now she could already have been here then.

'Nothing personal at all. I remember wondering whether to wait another week but the boy was going to the post for me anyway so I decided to send what there was: a catalogue, a letter requesting certain stones for a jeweller here — he'd left it here when he called and I said I'd send it on, and a letter from the Town Council. That was all.'

'Someone had ordered stones . . . would they be valuable ones?'

The goldsmith smiled at his ignorance.

'Of course. They were diamonds. But he would hardly have been bringing them down this week without letting me know, if that's what you're thinking. Besides, he wouldn't have had time to buy and cut them.'

'What about the letter from the Council?'

'I've no idea. Those yellow envelopes all look alike. A letter about the rates going up, a circular from the local library, or one of those offers of a free cancer test or X-ray from the department of health . . .' The goldsmith shrugged.

The Marshal had got to his feet and was toying with his hat. It was all there, he was convinced, if only he could grasp it; all the elements of a crime and all the elements of a family quarrel, too; but everybody kept telling him that there was no crime and no quarrel. Whenever he tried to grasp any one of the elements it evaporated like a ghost in daylight.

He sat down again with a thump and took out a handkerchief to mop his brow.

'And yet, *something* broke the family up . . . and why should he bring those dark clothes with him as if he were dressing for his own funeral . . .'

'There are those that say he was.'

'And are you one of them?' The Marshal stared up at him.

'No, I'm not,' he answered quietly, 'but it's for you to decide.'

'That's just what it isn't!' The Marshal's big hands were clenched on his knees in frustration, his face red with heat and a sort of aimless rage, like a bull too long tormented in the ring. 'That's just what it isn't—and I *know* that if I don't find the answer before he's buried I never will! Funerals—it always comes back to funerals.'

'Most family troubles do. That and money.'

'And this family seems to have had plenty of both—not to mention diamonds. If I could only feel I had more time I—'

He turned and recoiled from it before even hearing the blind man's warning bell and the boy's running footsteps.

Two inches away from him a white, malicious face was peering in through the hole in the paper.

CHAPTER 7

The face recoiled, too, in a second, and the Marshal had time to recognize both fear and surprise in its expression before it was gone and he was making for the door, colliding with the apprentice who was running in. Signor Beppe who, from his standing position, had seen nothing, hurried out after the Marshal and spotted the woman making for the corner almost at a run.

'Oh! Marshal!' he called out in surprise. 'But that's the Signora! Signora Goossens!'

But the Marshal, though he heard, didn't pause in his pursuit, and both he and the woman were soon out of sight round the corner.

'Now, Signora,' whispered the Marshal to himself. 'Now . . .' though he couldn't have said now what.

She had slowed down a little, once out of the square, and was walking at a normal pace along Via Mazzetta. She might not have known yet that she was being followed; even so, she was still walking a little too fast for this heat, which made her noticeable as she threaded through the lethargic shoppers and strolling tourists. On reaching the tiny Piazza San Felice, where four roads met in a tangle of blocked traffic, she glanced behind her, and the Marshal felt sure she saw him before hesitating a second and then turning left.

At first he thought she might be going to take another left turn and so arrive back in Piazza Santo Spirito, but instead she crossed over and took the fork that led to Pitti, disappearing for a moment among a crowd of Japanese tourists, the only people who were walking as briskly as she was. When he next spotted her she was in full sunlight, half way up the sloping forecourt in front of the palace.

It seemed, incredibly, that she must be making for the Station which lay beyond the archway on the far left, but after hesitating a moment by the postcard stall, she went in at the great central doors which led to the courtyard, the entrances to all the galleries, and the Boboli Gardens behind. She was immediately lost in the teeming gloom of the arcade. The Marshal, having panted up the slope behind her, had a moment of panic as the crowd sucked him in and his vision blurred. He had been too absorbed till then to notice that his sight had been getting steadily weaker, but now tears were rolling down his cheeks and he was as blind as a newly-emerged mole. Cursing himself, he plunged into his pockets in search of handkerchief and dark glasses. By the time he could see again he had little hope of spotting her, but the crowds worked in his favour rather than hers. She had rushed up the big staircase on the right that led to the Palatine gallery, and must have been turned away at the top of the four great flights because she had no ticket. The ticket office was down in the courtyard to the left of the stairs.

He spotted her trying to fight her way down through a coach party going up behind their leader who was waving a red handkerchief on a stick. The noise under the colonnade below was deafening, and two large women in pastel-coloured trouser suits were dragging at the Marshal's arm, shrilly demanding that he tell them the way to some incomprehensible place. He shook them off

and pushed his way towards the centre of the courtyard as
Signora Goossens had just done, and saw to his dismay
that she was making for the gardens beyond.

'Excuse me, excuse me!'

The walled-in stone path leading up to the level of the
gardens was narrow, and the over-heated tourists were
moving up at a snail's pace, probably grateful for a few
moments of shade. Excusing himself only caused them to
stop and stare at him, blocking his way more effectively.
A large young man in shorts swung round and hit him in
the face with an enormous, metal-framed backpack.

'*Excuse me*! Let me through, for the love of . . . !'

At last he was out at the top of the slope, under the
beating glare of the sun, with the cathedral dome shimmering beyond the trees. He spun round to the right,
sending up a spray of gravel, and saw the woman moving
quickly through a party of schoolchildren coming in the
opposite direction. If she had slowed down and mingled
with the crowd it would have been impossible to follow
her, but she went on pushing her way through them,
almost running.

'So, you're afraid of me,' muttered the Marshal under
his breath. He was already rather breathless and he felt
the gravel burning the soles of his shoes. In this open,
dusty space, the sun's intensity was sickening. The
Marshal had little enthusiasm for a chase through the
gardens. Having lived here so many years, she probably
knew them better than he did, and would undoubtedly
stick to this end where the crowds were always thickest.
There were at least three exits she could use . . .

'Now where are you going?' She was staying on the
lowest level and had taken the road that ran past the back
of the palace, then the left fork where a giant, glittering
white Pegasus reared up before a slope of clipped grass.
He lost her for a moment as she vanished round the bend
where a Roman sentinel marked the beginning of the

laurel walk. He quickened his pace, baffled. He had
assumed she had come in here either just to pose as a
tourist or to try and shake him off, but now he was
unsure. This part of the gardens was always quiet and she
must know that. It could be that her attempt at dodging
into the gallery had been a blind but that she had an
appointment here.

'Well, if you have, I'll come too, Signora, if you don't
mind . . .'

The covered laurel walks formed a maze of shady paths
on the side of a steep slope. Stopping at the bottom of the
first one and looking up the gravelled alley that seemed to
vanish into gloomy infinity, he spotted his quarry toiling
upwards and started after her. At the first intersection
her pale dress vanished among the dark green foliage to
the right. When the Marshal got there she was gone. He
stopped and took out a handkerchief to dry his forehead
and the back of his neck.

Except for the chinking of an amorous blackbird,
invisible in the dry grass and tangled shrubbery beyond
the confines of the covered walk, the garden was silent
and the Marshal listened to his own heavy breathing. He
would have liked to sit down on the stone bench he could
see jutting out a little further on, but his instinct told him
to keep going. He walked forward very slowly, listening
hard between the light crunch of his own footsteps. When
he came out momentarily into the light at the main intersection, he was so blinded, even behind dark glasses, that
the passage before him was a featureless black tunnel,
and only very gradually, as he walked through it, did its
roof of gnarled branches and the flecks of spent light on
the pathway reappear. Then he stopped.

He had heard a rustling noise accompanied by someone else's footsteps on the gravel. It came from somewhere along the path running parallel to the one he was
on. The Marshal peered through the tangle of sweet-

smelling leaves, past the grassy patch to the next walk, and spotted the movement of light-coloured clothing. There was no way of cutting through, so he hurried as quietly as he could to the end of his path, and climbed up to turn into the next one. The pale figure was still there.

'Good morning, Marshal. What brings you here? Not your day off, is it?'

'No, no . . . it isn't.'

The gardener who, in his rolled-up white shirtsleeves, was tying a small laurel sapling to a supporting pole, was the Marshal's next-door neighbour. He stopped work expectantly as the Marshal stood looking uncertainly about him.

'Another bag-snatcher, is it?'

'Not exactly. I wanted a word with a woman . . . a tourist . . . I thought I spotted her but it must have been you.'

'A fairly elderly woman? Wearing a sort of cream-coloured frock?'

'That's her.'

The gardener pointed with the clippers in his gloved hand. The scent of the bayleaves where he had been cutting and tying was almost overpowering.

'She's gone higher up. If you ask me, she's lost, but she couldn't be bothered to answer when I wished her good-morning, so I left her to it.'

The Marshal toiled heavily up to the next path. There was no one in sight along all its length. Sweat was pouring off him despite the shade of the branches bent overhead, and his shirt and the waistband of his trousers were soaked through. Again he spotted flecks of white among the dark green on some distant path and hurried forward, only to find a Roman matron smiling blindly down at him, one broken hand outstretched.

'Blast the woman!' muttered the Marshal without specifying whether the stone or the flesh and blood one.

He had reached the top of the 'maze' and he had lost her. There was nothing for it but to start down again. She may well have taken some other route but, since he had little or no hope of finding her, he might as well stay in the shade as brave the beating yellow glare on the open pathways. He took the steep walk going straight down the centre, his shoes sometimes skidding a little in the ochre dust of the gravel, and the gravel sometimes getting into his shoes.

At the bottom he paused by the fish pool, gazing across at the island. The still, green water was flecked with orange fish and edged with upside-down lemon trees in huge terracotta pots. The heat and silence were hypnotic, and he was almost going to sit down on a stone seat and close his eyes. It caused him physical pain to wrench his gaze from the green and gold vision and go on walking. It would help, he thought, if he could find some water to drink and get some of the dust out of his mouth. But when he moved towards the sound of trickling water and found, in a shady arbour, a moss-green man in jerkin and breeches emptying his ever-flowing wine jar into a barrel clutched by a grinning boy, the sign below the stone figures said 'Not drinking water'. With a sigh, the Marshal joined the tableau and held out his hands for the man to fill them with cool water which he dabbed on his head. He started back along one of the lower paths of the maze, pausing at the first intersection to listen.

As soon as his own footsteps ceased, he heard hers. They were coming towards him rapidly. She came round the corner from the path to his left and almost ran right into him. He stood there, still and apparently impassive behind his dark glasses, making the most of this first opportunity to have a look at her face. The eyes were cold and expressionless and the lips reduced to a thin dry line strangely crossed by vertical creases as though they had been mummified into an expression of selfish fury. Only a red blotch on her neck and an involuntary toss of her head indicated her nervousness as she swerved round him, startled, and hurried on down the slope, sending up little clouds of yellowish dust.

The Marshal pursued her doggedly, confidently. Having seen her close to, he realized that however inefficient his efforts at following her had been, she didn't know it. She looked as though she had been running all this time, convinced that he was cleverly shadowing her and managing to keep out of sight. He could almost have agreed with the gardener who had thought she was lost. Was it possible that in all her years in Florence she had never spent much time in the Boboli? It seemed so unlikely . . . the only green oasis among all that imprisoning stone . . . and yet she wasn't sure of her way . . . unless she was looking for somebody.

At the bottom of the slope she hesitated before turning right towards the palace. As they neared the crowded area where the tourists gathered, he got closer to her. It was nearing lunch-time, and people in shorts or flimsy sundresses were climbing up into the stone seats on the shady side of the amphitheatre and spreading out picnic meals, closely stalked by thin, wild-eyed cats. The cathedral bell, its tower visible beyond the trees, began to toll the Angelus and the Marshal began to wonder what was going to happen to his lunch.

As they came out through the courtyard and on to the car park he thought longingly of his cool, dark sitting-room, of taking off his sweaty uniform and dusty grit-filled shoes; of a shower and a meal and a doze in his arm-chair. But he went on following the woman, who had begun to look anxiously at her watch.

Where are we going now . . . ? the Marshal wondered, as she pushed her way along the narrow pavement of Via Guicciardini towards the Ponte Vecchio. He had already decided that he wouldn't like to be a tourist if they had to slog round like this all day. They crossed the bridge between the tiny jewellers' shops. Could she be going to see one of the jewellers? The Dutchman could easily have brought stuff with him, perhaps illegally imported . . . But the woman went straight across the bridge without so much as a glance at the shops, and now they were on the broader Por Santa Maria and she was looking at her watch again. If she did have an appointment, it hadn't been in Boboli where she had simply been trying to get rid of him.

At the flower market she turned right, into Via Vacchereccia, a short street which opened into the Piazza Signoria where the Palazzo Vecchio stood, the old palace with its crenellated top, heraldic shields and stone tower. Before going into the piazza the woman halted and looked again at her watch. The Marshal looked at his. It was after twelve. Still she was hesitating, trying now to look nonchalantly into the window of a big café on the corner, where handmade chocolates wrapped in thick yellow paper were stacked in little mountains. The Marshal wondered if she would go in, but after a glance at the prices on the tiny squares of chocolate, she went back a few yards and entered an ordinary bar.

The Marshal, watching her from the middle of the road said to himself, 'Good,' and followed her in. Even so, he thought, picking up a paper napkin and helping himself to a sandwich, it's a far cry from the international diamond business. It looks as though the saintly Signora doesn't like to part with her money. He ordered a coffee and a glass of water, and feeling in his top pocket for such money as he might find there, decided that it was just as well for him that she hadn't gone into the other place.

The narrow bar had only three tables in it, and Signora Goossens was sitting at one of them with two sandwiches and a cold drink.

'Have you a telephone?'

'In that little alcove at the back there.'

'Give me a token.'

From the alcove he was just able to see the two sandwiches and one of her shoes. He dialled, watching thin, claw-like fingers reach for one of the sandwiches and remove it from sight.

'Stazione Pitti.'

'Gino? Is that you?'

'Yes, Marshal. Where are you? Your dinner will—'

'I know, but I shan't be back. Share mine between you.'

They were always hungry. Gino had been known to down three bowls of *pastasciutta* before starting on his main course. 'Are there any messages?'

'Only one. A drug addict was arrested while trying to sell somebody a Fiat 500—it was the boy he was selling it to who was arrested first for pushing heroin, which was what he was going to pay with, but then the car turned out to be stolen, so for once we found a Fiat 500.'

'So what's the message?' The Marshal's surprise came through a mouthful of sandwich.

'The message is, will we look out for the owner because he hasn't reported it missing. Lorenzini says he probably never will because it wouldn't be worth much.'

'Have you checked—'

The second sandwich was still on the plate but the foot had vanished.

'Marshal . . . ?'

He hung up and ran for the door, dropping a thousand-lire note on the counter as he passed. If he'd been a second slower he would have lost her, but he spotted her cream-coloured dress and her too-rapid walk as she entered the Palazzo Vecchio. Then he slowed down to his usual steady pace. If they were going to play at being tourists again that was all right by him. The Palazzo Vecchio had only one public entrance and he would content himself to waiting beside it. Inside, tourists were milling about the dim courtyard, taking flash photographs of Verocchio's bronze cherub clutching his fat fish above the trickling water of the fountain, not minding, if they knew, that it was only a copy. From the left of the courtyard, office workers were streaming out from the part of the palace that was used as a town hall.

The two white-helmeted *vigili* on guard at the main doors looked curiously at the sweaty and dishevelled Marshal, but he wished them good-day without offering any enlightenment so they returned to their conversation, pausing now and then to direct visitors to the monumental apartments.

'It can't go on like this,' grumbled one of them, lifting his helmet to apply a handkerchief. 'It's like a Turkish bath. I haven't slept properly for three nights.'

'It won't go on,' said the other ominously, and a rumble of approaching thunder confirmed his prophecy.

Only then did the Marshal recall the blind flower man's words, 'There'll be a storm before long,' and he looked anxiously up at the sky. It was still innocently clear and blue, but there was more heavy dampness in the air than ever and the uneasy rumbling was now almost continuous. He glanced back into the courtyard just in time to see the woman coming out. When she saw him there she gave a tiny start and then turned and pretended to examine the bronze cherub and the water trickling from the fountain. Should he have followed her in, after all? It had seemed like just another ploy to dodge him, but if she had met someone . . . It was unlikely since she had only been in there for a few minutes . . . Even so, it was long enough, wasn't it, for something to change hands?

His eyes scanned the tourists coming out laden with cameras, rucksacks and guidebooks. He should have followed her in; she was much more agitated at his having found her there than she had been when she'd almost bumped right into him in the gardens. He stood there staring in at her, knowing that she felt it even though she kept her back to him. At last she made up her mind to move and came suddenly towards him, her shoulders stiff and straight but her head turned and lowered just slightly, despite her obvious efforts to keep it up. Once past him, she gave that little, nervous toss of the head again, almost as if she were saying, 'Whatever you may think, I have the right to do what I'm doing!' Yet there was something about her attitude, as the Marshal followed her across the piazza, that made him think she was both annoyed and frustrated. Had her meandering efforts to shake him off made her late for some appointment? Too late to do whatever she wanted to do? At the corner of Via de' Calzaioli she stopped. There was a newspaper kiosk there and she bought an English paper and stood a moment looking at it. The Marshal stationed himself in a doorway on the opposite side of the street and stared at such parts of her as were visible behind the open newspaper. He noticed that the heels of her cream shoes were thickish and not very high as the blind man had rightly judged. Were they the ones Signora Giusti had heard on the stairs? *It was a woman. High heels.* Well, they weren't very high, but high enough to distinguish them from a man's shoes. He wondered if she still wore the famous ring; or had that been discarded along with everything else belonging to her past life? From this distance he couldn't tell. How long were they to stay on this corner? She would have to make a move some time . . .

He glanced down the street towards the cathedral square where the bell tower stood. He looked harder. The bell tower was gone. He took off his dark glasses and stared at them before looking again down the street. He hadn't been deceived; there was no bell tower in sight. The lower half of the street had vanished in a thick, grey cloud, and the cloud was moving towards him, hissing with rain. People were fleeing before it, squealing and scattering into doorways, and the street was empty when the first great fork of lightning darted down into the centre of the road with an ear-splitting roar of rage. The cloud hadn't reached the piazza and the bit of sky directly over the Marshal was still blue. He looked around him for shelter, wondering if he could reach the Palazzo Vecchio, but the woman had stepped back under the awning of the kiosk and evidently intended to stay there.

The Marshal, too, stepped back, into a doorway which in itself offered little shelter but which at least had a high step and wooden eaves far above it that jutted out at least a metre from the building.

Even so, the rain, when it reached him, swept right over him and drenched him from head to foot, making him gasp. He pressed himself back into the doorway as far as he could, as the water swirled past beneath his feet. In the sudden darkness the street lights came on and then went off again as the lightning ripped down the side of one of the tall buildings. One or two taxis were still trying to crawl forward along Via de' Calzaioli with their head-lights on, but the rest of the traffic had stopped, and cars were temporarily abandoned in the middle of the road.

The woman was hidden from him now by a group of tourists in brightly-coloured transparent macs, who had joined her under the awning, squealing as the grey water ran in fast rivers round their ankles, and covering their plastic-hooded ears with their wet hands at each rending explosion that reverberated between the high buildings.

The Marshal knew the nature of this beast. After tearing at the great, hubristic dome of the cathedral, whose golden globe shone up at the clouds like a chal-lenge, it would flounder about the city, terrorizing the population and striking at everything in its path, then make for the high trees of the Boboli Gardens, moving steadily upwards to spend its fury finally bouncing from one to another of the hills surrounding the city, flashing and grumbling out there for the rest of the day and throughout the night, returning again and again to attack the red and white radio masts that bristled above the hill where the cemetery lay.

The lights came on again and stayed on. The Marshal wondered if the park-keepers had already started to evacuate Boboli, warning people to keep away from the trees, any one of which might be split open like matchwood. He remembered that he had left his bathroom window open . . . maybe he could get to a telephone before the storm reached Pitti . . .

A pair of flimsily-sandalled feet with bright red toenails came splashing through the water, and a breathless girl, her soaked dress clinging to her body, jumped on to the step beside the Marshal. She was carrying a waterlogged tray with three portable coffee cups and a pile of disintegrating sandwiches floating about on it. She had probably been on her way back to one of the dress shops with a snack lunch for her colleagues when she got caught. Water was streaming from her dark hair. After looking up and down the darkened street once or twice, she laughed up at the Marshal and said, 'What's the use?' Then she hopped out into the swirling water again and made off with her head down.

The Marshal's shoes had filled with water that had run down his drenched trousers. He tried to dry his face a little with a handkerchief but only succeeded in wetting the handkerchief. The rain which had been hot at first was now cooling and he began to shiver. Some of the tourists had made a run for it in their iridescent macs, and he could see Signora Goossens again now, her tinted hair lying flat and her face pale with fear, her chilly eyes regarding the storm with personal antipathy. Did she think it was some sort of divine retribution? If she did, she evidently considered it to be unjust . . .

'I have every right . . .' Right to what, though? What was she doing here after all these years? And if she did poison her stepson, what possible reason could she have had?

The lightning had moved on to the next street and was only visible as lurid flashes accompanied by deafening thunder that had already given the Marshal a piercing headache. The streetlights cast a livid gloom that was more dismal than the stormy darkness had been, and the sulphurous smell of the electrical discharge mingled with the earthy smell of the rainwater spouting from the terra-cotta roofs. The rain showed no sign of abating, and the fountains and drains were already overflowing. Water swilled over troughing in long sheets to hit the road far below with a loud clatter; waterfalls formed wherever there was a fault in a drainpipe, and grinning stone faces spewed malevolently into their flooded bowls.

People were calling to one another over the noise of the rattle and spray of the downpour; only the Marshal and the woman regarded each other silently from opposite sides of the street, and the look in her cold eyes was one of hatred.

'Marshal? Where are you?'

'In a bar.' This time he had her in full view as she stood dabbing at her hair with a handkerchief while waiting for a *caffelatte*. 'Listen, Gino lad, go through to my quarters, will you, and shut the bathroom window, if it's not too late to prevent a flood.'

'It's all right, we've already done it, sir. Lorenzini checked the whole building and put the board up in front of the cellar grating—he says it's going to be bad.'

'It is. Hasn't it reached you yet?'

'No, but it's very near; it's going dark . . .' Behind Gino's voice the Marshal could hear the loudspeakers in the Boboli Gardens giving out a warning in four languages. 'The electricity went off for a bit but it's on again now. Lorenzini said he hoped you were on this side of the river . . .'

'I'm not, but I'm not far away. I'll see you later.'

'You're not too far from home, I suppose? From your station?'

The blind man, like Lorenzini, had suffered in nineteen-sixty-six. In Florence, 'before the flood' had a more recent connotation than the biblical one, and each building carried a small ceramic plaque with a wavy line drawn on it at the height the water had reached on that November 4th. Some of the plaques were at second- and third-floor level.

The Marshal could feel the whole city tense and uneasy as he followed the woman wearily back across the Ponte Vecchio. Lights were on in the jewellers' windows and many of the shop-owners were standing in their doorways discussing the adequacy or inadequacy of the dredging and reinforcing of the river bed that was still going on. One of the big yellow diggers was marooned on an artificial sandbank, and people were hanging over the central parapet of the bridge to watch the racing brown water that was dragging along huge branches torn from trees far out in the country where the rain must have begun days ago.

The Marshal's only comfort, as he squelched miserably back along Via Guicciardini, was that Signora Goossens was as wet as he was; but since she was somewhat elderly and since he wasn't a vindictive man, it wasn't much comfort at all. Just before they reached Pitti, she turned in at a pensione on the left and he trudged mindlessly in after her. It was a place he had to call at, anyway, if he ever gave up this wild goose chase.

She had taken her key and vanished when he got up to the reception hall on the first floor of the building, and he made no effort to go after her, merely saying, as the non-plussed receptionist put the blue register into his dripping hand:

'I need to use your phone.'

He opened the register before dialling, and copied into his sodden notebook a British passport number and the name Goossens, Theresa. He didn't like her having his wife's Christian name, no matter how good she was supposed to have been. She had checked in the previous day, Tuesday.

'*Stazione Pitti.*'

'Gino? It's me again. I want you to tell Lorenzini to meet me immediately round the corner at the Pensione Giottino. I'm at the reception desk. If he doesn't find me here, he's not to worry but to go straight back to Pitti. Have you got that?'

'Pensione Giottino . . . yes, I've written it down. There's a message for you, Marshal; d'you want me to read it to you?'

'Go on.'

'A lady telephoned and said . . . I wrote it down because it sounded a bit odd . . . she said: "No, none of us, and I've checked the boys as well. Nobody." She said her name was Franca and that you'd know what she meant.'

'Yes. Thanks.'

He put the receiver down.

'That was no lady,' he muttered to himself, but he appreciated Franca's discretion and was amused by her having checked out the boys as well. He couldn't really imagine the Dutchman having picked up a prostitute at all, but the idea of his picking up one of the transvestites down the river . . . Even so, if you checked, you checked everything, otherwise there was no point.

'Is anything wrong, Marshal?' The receptionist, who did double duty as a porter, was observing him apprehensively.

'No,' the Marshal answered.

The one thing he had wanted to avoid was dragging

any of the lads into this business, but he couldn't go on in this soaked condition and he couldn't neglect his hotel round either.

He had to stand where he was until Lorenzini turned up because he was too wet to sit down in any of the cheap green armchairs in the reception hall. He had already made large black footprints and a spreading damp patch on the bit of carpet near the desk. Once again he noted with relief the Signora's reluctance to part with a lira; he would have been distressed to have to drip in the foyer at the Excelsior.

Lorenzini clattered up the stairs at a run, as he always did, his grey eyes bright with curiosity.

'This Signora here.' The Marshal pointed to the name on the register. 'If she comes out of her room the porter here — I'm sure he's paying attention although he's polite enough to be pretending not to — will tell you which is she. If she leaves I want you to follow her.'

'Follow . . .' Lorenzini's face dropped. 'Follow her? But . . . I mean . . . I'm not a detective!'

'What's that got to do with anything?'

'Well . . .' He looked down at himself. 'I'm in uniform, sir. She'll notice me. I mean, have I got to dodge in and out of doorways and stuff like that?'

'What the devil would you want to do that for?'

'Well . . . so she won't see me.'

The porter looked from one to the other like someone at a tennis match, his mouth slightly open. Both he and Lorenzini jumped when the Marshal exploded.

'What the devil does it matter whether she sees you or not! I want to know where she goes, that's all! *I want to know where she goes!* Do you understand me?'

'Yessir!'

'Just don't let her out of your sight!'

'Yessir!'

'And keep in touch with me. I'm going home. I'm wet!'

With this superfluous piece of information he stumped off down the stairs muttering, to the consternation of some guests on their way up, 'Dodge in and out of doorways, for the love of God . . . !'

The rain had eased off slightly and the Marshal was so wet anyway that he stumped round the rest of his hotel checks before going home, and gave the owner of the Pensione Giulia a piece of his mind for still not having found the date of issue of the Simmons passport, though still sure he'd 'jotted it down'.

'But Marshal, what if it was out of date, anyway? Really, what do you expect me to do? If people don't have their papers in order it's not my responsibility.'

'Your responsibility! You don't know the meaning of the word. But one of these days you'll be sorry. You'll be shouting for help and expect us to come running.'

'Well, anyway, it was only for one night, no harm done,' said the proprietor weakly.

And the Marshal exploded again.

When he finally got back to the Station, two hours later, Gino was in the office doorway, waiting for him. There were great pools of water in the gravel but the worst was over and he had taken away the board that stopped the cellar getting flooded.

'You're wet!' said young Gino in consternation. 'Marshal, I'd better tell you—'

'Gino, lad, whatever you want to tell me, let me in first.'

'But the thing is, Lorenzini telephoned and—'

'He's lost her! I'll break his neck, so help me!'

'No, sir, I mean no, he hasn't, but he said—'

'What are you whispering for?'

Gino glanced unhappily over his shoulder. 'He said to tell you that she took a taxi and he followed her and now he's at Borgo Ognissanti Headquarters and what is he to do—only that was over an hour ago . . .'

'He's where? And where the devil is the woman he's supposed to be following? Will you for goodness' sake let me in!'

When Gino still didn't move, the Marshal began to push him out of his way. He didn't notice the extra car parked beyond the van.

'But that's where she is, sir, or she was, and now there's an officer . . .'

The Marshal had pushed past him into the office. On the end of the table there was a slightly rain-spotted hat with a gold flame on the front of it and silver braid around it. In his chair, with a file in front of him and a gloved finger tapping slowly on the file, sat the young Lieutenant, his face pale and his lips pursed.

CHAPTER 8

The Marshal had never been happier. The Goossens file was open on the desk in front of him, its contents spread out, and he was scribbling fast on a sheet of foolscap. Below the tall window, cars came and went, their sirens starting up or winding down as they reached the electronic gates of Headquarters. After the storm, the last hours of sunshine had seemed like a new day, and the sky was wide and clear as it turned pink. When, occasionally, the door of the operations room opposite opened to let out a burst of noise, the Marshal didn't look up from his work but a look of satisfaction crossed his face. He felt the computers were whirring for his benefit. The Lieutenant had gone across to make contact with the French authorities and check on the date when Signora Goossens crossed the Channel. The Marshal, who had joined up well before everything had become so computer-orientated, would have liked to go with him but he was afraid of being in the way or of touching something he shouldn't. The boys in there looked hardly more than students to him and he had said to himself, as he glanced in there in passing, 'By God, but we get some educated lads, these days!' He felt as proud of them as if they had been his own children.

There was a knock at the door and a carabiniere came in with two cups of coffee and some biscuits on a tray.

'Lieutenant Mori ordered these, sir.'

'Thanks. Let me move these papers and you can put the tray down here.'

He sat back in his chair for a moment sipping the coffee. The lad who had brought it had been young and pink-faced and had reminded him of Gino. He smiled, as everyone always did, at the thought of Gino, of his frightened face when the Marshal and the Lieutenant had emerged from the office and found him still trying to disperse the floodwater in front of the entrance. It was the face children have when their parents quarrel and they are helpless to intervene. The Marshal had patted his shoulder on the way out, wanting to tell him, 'It's all right, lad.'

Because it had been all right. The Lieutenant, after a rambling and embarrassed preamble, had eventually announced that Signora Goossens had been to see him, and the Marshal had braced himself, his mind already groping for an explanation to offer—not to the Lieutenant but to his own wife after his sudden transfer. He hadn't thought at the time that he had been risking so much, but the Lieutenant's embarrassment, his reluctance to say what he had to say, made him think that things were much more serious than he had expected. He found it difficult to concentrate on what was being said to him as he sat there looking down at his large, clasped hands, his face red. Eventually, because the Lieutenant turned and spoke more directly, urgently to him, a clear sentence reached his troubled consciousness.

'There was something about that woman—Signora
Goossens—that I found deeply disturbing; I felt she was
hiding something—but then, why should she come and
see me? I felt a sort of defiance in her attitude, as if she'd
done something but was convinced she had the perfect
right . . . I don't know exactly how to put it, Marshal, but
I feel sure that if you'd seen her . . .'

There was enough of a pause for those last words to
sink in, and for the Marshal to start pulling himself
together. She hadn't made a complaint. She hadn't
dared, then. She had pretended not to know she was
being followed and had presented herself at Headquarters
to put herself in the right. It always seemed to come back
to that . . . 'I have the right' . . . and the Lieutenant had
noticed it, too, and been equally baffled by it.

'All the time she was talking to me, her eyes were
darting about as if she thought someone might pop out of
a cupboard and arrest her. I can't think who . . .'

The Marshal was silent.

'She admits . . . says . . . that she was here to see her
stepson, though she hasn't seen him in ten years, but I
couldn't very well force her to tell me why; she would only
say it was a private family matter, chiefly concerning
herself, and could have no bearing on the suicide . . .'

'She actually *said* suicide?'

'Yes. But I had already mentioned the Substitute
Prosecutor's feeling on the matter, so . . . I really can't see
why she should have been so nervous. The way she kept
glancing at the door you'd think she was afraid someone
had followed her to my office . . .'

The Marshal stared at his wet shoe.

'I see that you think I'm exaggerating. I'll confess something to you: this is my first case . . . the first I've dealt
with on my own . . .'

The Marshal arranged his features in an expression of surprise.

'Yes,' insisted the Lieutenant, 'it is.'

How old would he be? Twenty-four or -five? He looked younger. Perhaps because he had freckles. Underneath them, his face flushed slightly, annoyed with himself, probably, for having dropped his guard, for forgetting that he was an officer talking to a humble Marshal, behaving instead like a nervous youngster asking a more experienced man for help. The Marshal's heart went out to him for that blush, but he couldn't tell him what he wanted to know without unloading on to his young shoulders the responsibility for his own unauthorized activities. Instead, he asked:

'Have you spoken to the Substitute Prosecutor?'

'This evening, briefly, before coming here.'

'And what does he say?'

'He . . . he's already sent in his application to the Instructing Judge for an *Archiviazione* under "No action required".'

'I see.'

'I rather thought that you . . . that when you came to see me yesterday morning you were of the opinion . . .'

'That the Dutchman had been murdered, sir. Yes.'

'I naturally looked into the matter carefully, and there are one or two things that don't quite fit with the usual sort of suicide. If anything further happens to come to your notice . . .'

'One or two things have, sir.'

'The Instructing Judge won't sign the *Archiviazione* until after the funeral in case a complaint should be brought by a member of the family. That means we have until about lunch-time tomorrow . . .'

'We can only do our best then, sir, can't we? If you wouldn't mind . . . I think I ought to get changed . . .'

It was only then that the Lieutenant noticed that the

Marshal's uniform was soaked.

Now it was a little after eight-thirty in the evening and the light outside was dissolving into dusk. The Marshal finished his coffee and switched on the Lieutenant's desk lamp. It seemed they now had an hour longer than they had expected. The Dutch Consulate had telephoned to say they had a message from the Dutchman's mother-in-law; the baby had been born at five this morning, a boy, two weeks premature. As a consequence of the onset of her daughter's labour, the mother-in-law had not caught the train last night as planned but had taken the Holland-Italia express this afternoon. This train would not arrive in Florence until ten-thirty-six tomorrow, so the funeral had been put back an hour to eleven-thirty. The goldsmith, Signor Beppe, had taken charge of all the arrangements as soon as the body had been released by the Medico-Legal Institute. The Dutchman was now lying in his coffin in the goldsmith's front studio which had been cleared for the purpose and decorated with the blind man's flowers and two beeswax candles.

'Better here,' the goldsmith had said when the Marshal and the Lieutenant had called to pay their respects on the way over to Headquarters, 'than up there.' His eyes looking momentarily at the ceiling. 'I never knew him unhappy in this room.'

They hadn't disagreed with him.

'Marshal.' The Lieutenant hurried into the room now with a slip of paper in his hand which he put before the Marshal without a word before sitting down at his own side of the desk.

'Well, we had to expect that, Lieutenant,' said the Marshal after glancing at the slip. 'Nobody would be foolish enough to lie about it, not after filling in an embarkation card.'

'I know.' The Lieutenant rubbed at his eyes with fingers taut with nervousness. 'It's just that we're so pressed for time that every dead end has to be counted in minutes wasted.'

In the Marshal's experience, checking the obvious was an important part of any inquiry, but now was hardly the time to say so.

'I've made a list of everything we know,' he said. 'And of all the people in any way involved—perhaps we should start with the sequence of events as far as we know it. If you like, I'll read it out and you can think.'

'Go ahead.' The Lieutenant looked up through his fingers.

'Right. The Dutchman was last here four months ago and we know from Signor Beppe that at some point during that visit he said his stepmother—whom he hasn't seen for about ten years—must come back now. He didn't say why. What a lot of trouble he might have saved us if he had. After he left, his mail was sent on to him but there seems to have been nothing of note among it—in any case, Signora Goossens says she came to Florence having arranged to meet her stepson by letters going between England and Amsterdam. So the Dutchman sets off for a trip to Florence, telling his wife it was a business trip. Signor Beppe and Signora Giusti both say the wife is anti-stepmother since she has never met the woman and only knows her as someone who caused her husband a lot of upset when she disappeared. Presumably that's why he didn't tell her the real reason. He caught the Holland-Italia express that leaves Amsterdam at eight-nineteen in the evening and which should have arrived in Florence at sixteen-thirty-three the following afternoon, that was Sunday. In fact—' he checked his notes against the details provided by the station-master—'the train was delayed nineteen minutes in Basle because of the derailment of a goods train, and having then missed its turn at every station after that it lost more time and eventually arrived in Florence at four minutes to seven. We know from what he ate that he called at at least two places to get food. We could check on that if need be. Cold meat and cheese, etcetera, he could only have got from a meat-roaster because it was Sunday. The coffee he could have bought from any number of bars.'

'For that we would need a recent photograph of him which we don't have.'

'Signora Giusti might well have one in her album. We can't get in to see her now, she'll be in bed, but perhaps tomorrow . . .

'Now, he didn't call on Signora Giusti when he got to the flat—that could have something to do with keeping the assignment a secret but it could just be that it would be after her bedtime by then and he had no good reason for disturbing her—she's always in bed by half past seven. The mysterious woman arrived towards eight. We can assume she had eaten because she didn't eat with the Dutchman—at least, I hardly think she could have cleared up after herself and not after him; it would have looked too odd. Perhaps she made the famous jug of coffee while he was eating. It's likely, because, judging from where his plate was found on the table as I remember it, he would have had his back to her as she worked at the sink and the cooker.'

The Lieutenant thought a moment and then said:

'That would suggest somebody familiar; it certainly doesn't sound as if it were a prostitute . . .'

'It wasn't. I've checked. One of them could be lying, of course, but I don't see why a prostitute should want to kill him.'

'To rob him? He could have been carrying stones, even illegally . . .'

'In that case she'd have had to stay around until he went to sleep and rob him, not quarrel with him and leave. According to Signora Giusti she left immediately following the quarrel. Later there was a lot of crashing

about — that would be the Dutchman searching the bathroom, possibly looking for the aspirin bottle from which,
at some point, he'd taken a couple of pills, thinking he'd
made a mistake and taken something poisonous. Then
nothing till I found him, but the pathologist tells us he
had vomited the first dose, or some of it and, having slept
off most of the rest,he woke up and took more of the
coffee, whether purposely or accidentally we can't be
sure. The unknown woman has vanished into thin air,
and if she did steal anything we don't know what. Legally
imported stones would mean documentation to go with
them and copies in his office at home, but no such
documentation exists. A registered importer has no
reason to fool about carrying stuff illegally because it
wouldn't be worth his while according to Signor Beppe,
and it certainly seems reasonable. She could have stolen
something else, of course, like a compromising letter, but
he doesn't sound the type for it, and again, she would
surely have had to wait until he was safely asleep.
Anyway, she vanishes on Sunday night. On Tuesday
Signora Goossens arrives in Florence, oddly enough on
that same train which has carriages coming from most
northern European cities . . . She books in at the Pensione
Giottino. She has an appointment with her stepson but
she isn't saying why. That's all wrong!'

'What is?' The Lieutenant roused himself from con-
templation.

'Well, if . . . when did she say this appointment was
for?'

'Well, she didn't. Naturally since he was dead when
she arrived . . .'

'I wonder who told her?'

The Lieutenant reached for the annotated sheet of
foolscap and frowned at it.

'You see what I mean, apart from that? If they had an
appointment for Wednesday, or even Tuesday evening,

why should the Dutchman leave home on Saturday to be here on Sunday? Especially as he was supposed to have no other real business here and his wife was annoyed at his leaving her. The letter from his stepmother agreeing to the appointment or asking for it . . . ?'

'It wasn't among his things here and his mother-in-law was unable to find any clue to the reason for his visit among his papers at home. It's more than likely that he got rid of it, given that he was being secretive about the whole business. So, if Signora Goossens didn't get here until Tuesday, the day after he died, if there really was a woman in the flat with him as we think, then he must also have had an appointment with her, not just with his step-mother — after all, she couldn't have found him at the flat by chance, I don't suppose, given that he only spends a few days a year there. This may mean that Signora Goossens doesn't come into the thing at all, just as she says . . .'

They were both silent for a moment, thinking of the pale, tight-lipped face, the defiant look of righteousness.

'I don't believe it,' said the Marshal stubbornly, glowering at the print-out of her embarkation card. He thumped the table with his big fist and then remembered where he was.

'Excuse me, Lieutenant . . .'

'That's all right. I feel the same way, but there's no getting round the facts. You're certain the man said nothing else before he died?'

'Not a word. It's a wonder he managed to say what he did. Even so, it wasn't much help because if we ever did find the mysterious woman visitor we'd be faced with his having said, "It wasn't her," which would leave us back at square one.'

'If it was true, it would . . . but, you know, since he was expecting his stepmother, and since no one knew about his meeting this other woman, he might have been afraid of our suspecting Signora Goossens — which, in fact, we did — and he was just trying to protect her.'

'I suppose he could, but I don't think . . .' The Marshal frowned, remembering the Dutchman's voice and the way one sightless eye had opened as he died. 'If he'd been capable of thinking that out, and I don't honestly think he was, he'd have been capable of being clearer, of saying it wasn't my stepmother, or something of that sort. No, I'm sure it wasn't that. And then—I may not have told you, but it was one of the *Misericordia* Brothers who remarked on it—he sounded *surprised*. Why should that be?'

'Surprised?' The Lieutenant rapped his fingers on the desk. 'Well . . . if he was surprised that it wasn't her, it can only mean he thought it should have been her because she was the only person he'd seen.'

'That's true . . . and obviously he didn't think of the coffee, or he wouldn't have drunk more of it. Well, I suppose that must be it, then.'

'You don't sound very convinced, Marshal.'

'No . . . no, I'm sure you're right . . . it's just that he didn't say it in exactly that tone . . . but I expect you're right.'

The Lieutenant regarded him for a moment but the Marshal's bland expression gave nothing away. Even so, he was cautious enough to ask:

'You don't have any other ideas as to why he might have said it?'

'Well, only the obvious one.'

'Which is?'

'That the woman wasn't who he'd thought she was.'

'That's a great help! We don't know who she was and now we have to guess who he *thought* she was!'

'I realize it's not much help . . .' The Marshal's great eyes rolled around the room which was all in darkness now except for the pool of white light on the Lieutenant's littered desk. 'It's just that it seemed the obvious reason . . . I mean, it couldn't have meant it wasn't she who poisoned him, could it? If he'd done it himself he could have said so or left a note, and he couldn't have thought it was anyone other than this woman because he hadn't seen anybody else.'

'As far as we know.'

'That's true. As far as we know . . .' The Marshal looked down at his notes. 'I suppose this isn't what you could call evidence; it's only hearsay and general information really.'

'Exactly. Most of it depends on people having told the truth, and I can name at least one among them,' pointed out the Lieutenant, 'who's much given to telling elaborate lies.'

'Signora Giusti? It's true that a lot of this information came from her. Did she tell *you* lies?' The Marshal was truly astonished. He couldn't believe that she would dare treat an officer in the way that . . .

'She told me the Council social worker had tried to rob her.'

'She did? What of?'

'Her burial money—I promised not to tell anybody it existed, but really . . . Apparently she came into the bedroom and found this young woman with her hands under the mattress.'

'And she couldn't have just been making the bed as she does every day, I suppose.'

'Of course not. Attempted robbery. She may also, I understand, be attempting a slow poisoning job as well.'

'I see.' The Marshal began to realize that, by virtue of his mature years and the profiteroles, he had got off lightly. 'Nevertheless, the Dutchman's family seems to have brought out the best in her—such as it is—I'm almost convinced that what she's told us about them is the truth, unless . . .'

'Unless?'

'I was thinking that, if it's not, then she's been very clever. She might have invented the mysterious woman . . . though

of course, that was before we went in there, before she knew
anyone was dead.'

Or was it? The Marshal could see the wicked old
woman chuckling maliciously among her cushions, see
her with the Dutchman's keys in her hand, see her rattling
along the corridor saying, before she'd seen anything at
all, 'What have you found? Is somebody dead?' And in
the Dutchman's hands were her keys. It had been easy to
assume that he had been going to Signora Giusti for help,
but how did they know that he hadn't just come back
from there, or was about to return there, after a previous
visit, to find out what she had given him that could have
made him ill?

'Is something the matter, Marshal?'

'I . . . I'm trying to stop thinking about Signora Giusti
as just an old woman, as someone not to be considered.
It's what we do to old people, as if their age made them
less than human, less than an individual. And it was
Signora Giusti herself who warned me against it. She likes
attention, you see . . . not popularity, just attention.'

'You surely don't think . . . ?'

'Why not?'

'Well, because . . .'

'Because she's old. That's what I'm trying to explain,
Lieutenant. I know I'm not expressing myself very well. I
was never a great brain . . .'

*The old keyhole, lower down. You should be able to see
the entire house through it.*

Had she seen something? Had there, in fact, been
another woman?

*If he came back, the first thing he would do would be
to come and see me.*

And if he hadn't? Could the poison have been meant
for the woman, whoever she was, and the Dutchman have
died by mistake?

'Surely,' the Lieutenant pointed out, 'it's simply that at

her age she could have nothing to gain?'

'At her age she has nothing to lose. As for what she might gain, we really don't know that . . . revenge, jealous satisfaction, even a small legacy.'

'I know about that,' said the Lieutenant. There was a photostat of the will, obtained from the Dutchman's solicitors, in the file before them. 'But you don't murder an old friend for a couple of million lire. Even if she could get about, she wouldn't get very far on that. It might buy her a few new clothes, I suppose.'

The Marshal thought for a moment and then said quietly, 'It would bury her.'

'What?'

'It would bury her. Probably that's what it's for. It's the only thing, I think, that matters to her now.'

He could feel her tiny fingers clutching desperately at his arm.

What will happen to my poor old bones?

'She cared about being buried respectably, all right. I wonder . . . Do we have the number of the goldsmith? His home number, I mean?'

'Yes, we do. There is the list at the back of the file.'

'We might ring him, I think, sir, if you agree . . .'

'Go ahead. I can't say I share your suspicions but you're right in saying that we shouldn't ignore her as a possible suspect. It won't be difficult, anyway, to find out whether she had sleeping pills or any of this Viennese coffee, since she can't get out to buy anything for herself — really, Marshal, you must admit she's a pretty unlikely suspect. Even if she knows nothing at all about police laboratories and the like, she must have known we'd find her out.'

'Only if we stopped treating her as an old woman of no importance. And she called us,' the Marshal said as he dialled. 'She called us twice. And when I got there she kept me talking for over an hour before telling me there was something wrong next door. And what if we did find her out? What would we do about it? She'd perhaps be put in a home for the senile but would anybody take her legacy off her, knowing what it was for? She'd still get a respectable resting-place for her bones. Funerals!' The Marshal slapped a hand down on his knee. 'Funerals, quarrels and diamonds! It's all there, if only . . . Hello? Signor Beppe? Excuse me for disturbing you at home. Marshal Guarnaccia speaking . . .'

'Ah! Good evening, Marshal. And were you able to speak to her?'

'Speak to . . . ?'

'Signora Goossens! you went off after her in enough of a—'

'Ah yes . . . I . . . ah . . .' He could feel the Lieutenant's eyes on him and he kept his own averted. 'It was another matter I wanted to ask about.'

He hadn't thought at the time, but it was fortunate that the Lieutenant had let him make the call himself, otherwise . . .

'You mentioned that in his will the Dutchman left a small legacy to Signora Giusti.'

'That's right, yes. Nothing much because she's very old, you know, and it didn't seem likely, he thought, that she would live to claim it . . . he was wrong about that, God rest his soul. If she'd had any descendants, of course, he'd have left her something more substantial, but under the circumstances . . .'

'Yes . . . Tell me, was he a generous man, would you say?'

'Generous? I've already told you how much I owe to him. They were all of them generous, his father the same.'

'And his stepmother?'

'And his stepmother, too. Exceptionally so.'

'I see. I was just wondering about Signora Giusti . . . she seems to have had to sell most of her furniture, so . . .'

'So you wondered why Toni never helped? Well, I can tell you that. He did. But she wouldn't knowingly take a penny off him, not a penny. She's a rum old creature and she's proud. She was once pretty well off, you see, when her husband was alive, so the idea of accepting charity was one she couldn't stomach at any price. What Toni did was to make arrangements with the social worker to have her bills paid through his bank, and he pays for her to go to a place out in the hills in summer so she doesn't suffer the worst of the heat. I suppose she imagines it's free.'

'She knows nothing about these arrangements?'

'Not as far as I know. She may have had a suspicion and turned a blind eye, I couldn't say. Nevertheless, every now and then, when she wants some ready cash for any reason, she sells bits of her furniture, getting practically nothing for it, of course, needless to say, but no one can stop her.'

'Did she know about the legacy?'

'Oh, I should think so. I mean, that was the point of it, to give her some peace of mind. She has this idea, you see, that there's nobody to bury her with her having no family left. Naturally, Toni promised to see to everything, but she was still terrified that nobody would let him know, or that something would happen to him before she died; hence the legacy. It's just enough to give her a decent burial. Even so, she's forever trying to make alternative arrangements, just in case. She doesn't know, for instance, that I know anything about the will or about Toni's having promised to see to things, and she's made me promise that I'll arrange her funeral. She has this bit of money under the mattress . . .'

The Marshal couldn't help smiling.

'Does she think it's enough?'

'You know about it, then?'

'The same way that you do.'

'Then you know what I mean. Goodness knows how many people are going to be arranging her funeral! As for whether she thinks it's enough money, it's difficult to say, really. Remember that, these days, she has no contact with the outside world and that it must be impossible for her to realize how little her money's worth. Just think what you would have been able to buy with a hundred thousand lire in her day . . .'

'I can imagine.'

'Even so, she must have noticed the cost of some things and be worried about it. She told me that there was still the rest of the furniture to sell, if necessary. The house isn't hers.'

'Who owns it?'

'Toni; his widow now. It came up for sale five years or so ago and Toni bought it. There was always the danger that a new owner would try to evict her or at least put up the rent to the current level which she couldn't possibly have paid. He planned to sell it again after she died.'

'I see. Well, thank you. I don't think there's anything else.'

'Glad to be of service. Is there any further news about what exactly happened to Toni?'

'Not really. Is there someone with the body?'

'We got a woman in for the night and I'll take over early tomorrow morning. Will you be at the funeral?'

'Yes, I think I will, and so will Signora Goossens—you don't happen to know, do you, who told her about the Dutchman's death? It wasn't you?'

'Me? You know I only got a glimpse of her. I must admit I thought she'd have been in touch with me by now, but she hasn't. I imagine anyone in the piazza could have told her. There were a couple of lines in yesterday's paper, too, of course. Do you know where she's staying? She's not in the flat, I've been up and knocked. Not that I blame her . . .'

'She's at the Pensione Giottino in Via Guicciardini.'

'Right. I'll give her a ring about the arrangements for tomorrow.'

'Thank you again, and excuse my disturbing you . . .'

'Don't mention it.'

The Marshal replaced the receiver and met the Lieutenant's expectant gaze.

'Well,' he said, 'I was right about the legacy. It is for her funeral. But she had alternative arrangements. Nevertheless, it might be as well to have a look round her flat and a word with the social worker. It can't be done now, of course, she'll be asleep. But tomorrow . . .'

'I'll see what I can do. But it will be difficult, if not impossible, to get a search warrant.' The younger man blushed at his own powerlessness, but what he said was true.

'It may not be necessary,' pointed out the Marshal blandly. 'I should think a word with the social worker when she arrives tomorrow will be enough to tell you whether she might have had the sleeping pills and the peculiar coffee—or at least the coffee; the pills she could have had tucked away for years. I'll go to the funeral; it's my day off.'

'Not a pleasant way to spend it.'

'But I'll go, all the same. Without having actually known him, I feel I liked that Dutchman. His name was really Ton . . .'

'Do you have any further notes to read out?'

'Just this list of all the people concerned. I'm not sure why I wrote it down except that all the stories Signora Giusti told me left me more confused than enlightened. That may have been deliberate, of course, if she—'

'Shall we hear the list?'

'Right, sir. First, the Dutchman himself—father Dutch, mother Italian, both deceased. The stepmother, Signora Goossens—it's generally agreed that they were all very happy together but that after old Goossens's death she left for England and never saw her stepson again. Yesterday she arrived here to meet him — I think we're going to have to find out why if we want to make any headway — but in any case, he was dead before she entered the country. Signor Beppe, in the Dutchman's debt, a life-long friend, doesn't benefit in any way we know of from the Dutchman's death; was a witness to the will — who was the other, do we know?'

'Another craftsman from the same studio, an old friend of his father's, died three years ago.'

'Right, that only leaves Signora Giusti . . . well, we've been through all that. At the Amsterdam end there's his wife and his mother-in-law who's a widow. Do you think you'll get a chance to talk to the mother-in-law tomorrow?'

'There's a meeting arranged for after the funeral in the Substitute Prosecutor's office with the Dutch Consul or his representative. I shall be there but I somehow doubt she'll have anything further to say. Besides which, I feel that this whole thing turns on something that happened here, whether now or ten years ago, and that these people in Amsterdam don't come into it at all. I could be completely wrong, of course . . .'

'For what it's worth, sir, I agree with you. I know I'm not really competent in these matters and we have nothing to offer the Substitute Prosecutor who is. I'd just like to know what makes him so sure it's suicide. Even Professor Forli had doubts after all . . .'

'He did?'

'Well I — I get the impression he did from the wording of his report. The mention of the aspirins, for instance . . .'

'Well, it's easy enough to have doubts, and to be fair to him, I think the Substitute Prosecutor has them too, because of the aspirin and because there was no note. But as far as he's concerned, his doubts lead him to believe in accidental death instead of suicide. He's not even considering other possibilities, he has no reason to. There's no motive for murder, no suspect, no clue, not even any clear fingerprints on that coffee-pot, and no witnesses unless you count Signora Giusti who is not only elderly and infirm but also given to lying. Even if we believe her we're left with the fact that the Dutchman was alive after the mystery woman left and even took a further dose next day.'

He didn't add that the Substitute Prosecutor had virtually accused him of trying to exaggerate this, his first case, for his own glory, and had treated him with evident irony, but the Marshal strongly suspected as much.

The lights had come on in the warm street below, which meant it was nine-twenty or so. A mosquito landed on the papers strewn about under the desk lamp, dodging off again when the Marshal lifted his hand.

'So there it is,' said the Lieutenant, 'unless there's anyone else on your list?'

'No . . .' But should there have been? He had meant it about Signora Giusti confusing him; the characters she had paraded before him, English, Dutch and Italian, most of them long dead, had become so muddled in his head that it was difficult to disentangle Signora Giusti's own relations from those of the Dutchman. He felt there was somebody missing, and yet the goldsmith had been sure that, other than his wife, stepmother and mother-in-law, the Dutchman had nobody. He looked at his list again and then let his eyes ramble tiredly over the contents of the file. There was a coloured snapshot among them, the one taken from the Dutchman's wallet; a picture of his young wife sitting in a garden with an Alsatian dog beside her. She was smiling very prettily for the camera. Her forehead was high and smooth, and her hair, as Professor Forli had remarked, so blonde as to appear almost white. Now she must be lying in a hospital somewhere up there in the north. What would be going through her mind as she lay awake in those antiseptic surroundings? A new mother with no husband. Or would they have given her something to make her sleep?

'If you're sure there's nobody else,' the Lieutenant's voice interrupted, though he, too, was looking at the snapshot, 'we may as well go downstairs and have a sandwich and then I'll get someone to drive you back over to Pitti.'

'I'd as soon walk over, sir; stretch my legs. But the sandwich would be welcome.'

In the bar on the courtyard downstairs, the carabiniere who served them knew the Lieutenant's habits and poured him out a small glass of beer to drink with his sandwiches before saying:

'And for you, Marshal?'

It would never have occurred to him to drink beer, but he felt like being companionable and ordered the same.

'A northern habit.' The younger man raised his glass. 'Your health, Marshal.'

There were no other customers and the barman turned his radio on at full volume. The bluish fluorescent light, the immaculate tiled floor and the neat rows of bottles had a desolate air about them at this time of night when the night patrol cars had gone out and everything had fallen silent.

'I've got a northern lad at Pitti,' the Marshal said to fill the emptiness.

'Of course! One of the boys from Pordenone!'

'You know them?'

'Everybody's heard of them. I don't know them personally, though I've seen them together. A friend of mine teaches at the NCO school, Lieutenant Cecchi; he told me about them. It seems they spend every free minute they've got together. They don't really come from Pordenone, you know, but from right out in the wilds. Pordenone must have been the only town they'd seen until they enlisted. At any rate, when they first arrived here, everything they saw was compared to "the one in Pordenone" and the name stuck to them. Odd, when they're so inseparable, that they didn't apply for admission to the school together.'

'I can't persuade the lad,' said the Marshal unhappily. 'He just doesn't have any ambition for the future.'

'Well, if I were you, I'd keep trying. Cecchi says the brother's doing well. Now, I suppose we may as well call it a day. If you think of anything, anything at all, give me a ring. Otherwise, I'll see you in Piazza Santo Spirito tomorrow morning. I can't honestly say that I'm looking forward to another *tête-à-tête* with Signora Giusti . . .'

'If you think it would be of any help, I'll come along early and go up with you.'

'It might help a lot; she seems to think well of you—but it is your day off, after all.'

'If I'm going to the funeral . . .' The Marshal shrugged.

'Well, if you're sure. What time does the social worker get there?'

'I should think that if we make it half past nine, she should be there by then.'

'I still feel we may be harassing a very old lady unnecessarily.'

'It might turn out to be unnecessary,' persisted the Marshal calmly, 'but you needn't worry, sir, that she'll feel harassed. As I said, she likes attention.'

'Even so, I must say I'd rather we had something on this Signora Goossens that everyone insists is such a paragon of virtue.'

'It's hard to believe it,' agreed the Marshal, 'with that hard and tight-lipped face . . .'

'But . . . you've seen her, then?'

'No, no,' lied the Marshal placidly, 'I'm just going on your description, sir, that's all.'

'I see. You're sure you prefer to walk home?'
'Quite sure.'

Again, before leaving he assured the Lieutenant that if
anything important occurred to him he would telephone,
no matter what the hour. Something did occur to him
and the hour was three-fifteen in the morning. He didn't
telephone because, whether it turned out to be important
or not, nothing could be done about it then, if there was
anything that should be done at all. He had woken suddenly, not groggy but wide awake, as though it were time
to get up. Although he had no recollection of it, his brain
must have been ticking over while he slept and the person
missing from his list last night had clicked into place and
woken him up. Even though he was so wide awake he was
afraid he might forget again, so he rolled over and
switched on the lamp by the telephone where there was a
notepad. On it he wrote: 'The sister.' Then he went back
to sleep.

CHAPTER 9

When the alarm clock went off at eight, an hour later
than usual, the Marshal was already awake, his mind
ticking faster than the clock as he lay staring across at the
photo of his little boys on the chest of drawers facing him.

'Two of them,' he said aloud, referring not to the little
boys but to Signora Goossens and her sister. 'One who
arrived on Tuesday and the other who arrived . . . when?
On Sunday or earlier, I suppose. Two of them, blast
them! What the devil were they up to? What sort of hold
had the Dutchman over them that he could make them
come out here after all these years? Whatever it was, they
killed him for it. Or one of them did—not this one,

Signora Goossens, they'd checked on when she came over, and two people had identified her, the neighbour who saw her going downstairs and Signor Beppe. She was out of it then, as far as the actual poisoning was concerned, but they must surely have worked the thing together, getting him to keep an appointment at which he expected to see his stepmother. That's why he said it wasn't her, because it was the sister. They quarrelled violently . . . what about? About whatever they quarrelled over ten years ago . . . the thing nobody will tell me about. Everybody swears there was no quarrel but, damn it, all families quarrel! Why shouldn't this one? Maybe it was a quarrel that involved them all, the studio and Signor Beppe, old Signora Giusti, all of them, and nobody dares speak out. It's hopeless . . .'

He got up and started to get himself ready. As he was shaving his temper rose at the thought of so many people deceiving him to cover something up. Especially at the thought of Signor Beppe. He could have sworn that Signor Beppe was an honest man, and yet he was so insistent that Signora Goossens was good and generous, that although she left after the funeral without a word, there had not been any quarrel. He said there couldn't have been because Toni was in Amsterdam at the time—

The Marshal cut himself.

'And it's no more than you deserve,' he growled at himself as he scrabbled in the bathroom cabinet for a styptic pencil, tumbling things out as the Dutchman had done. 'In Amsterdam, indeed! So why wasn't he at his own father's funeral? Because that's the way it sounds, if the woman left immediately . . . And there hadn't been a row? He may have found a girl-friend up there but you don't miss your own father's funeral for that!'

That meant that the quarrel must go back to before old Goossens's death . . . perhaps to the time when Toni decided to go and work up there. Giving up the search for the styptic pencil, he stuck a scrap of newspaper over the cut and carried on getting dressed.

When he went into the front office, Gino was at the switchboard.

'Good morning, Marshal.'

' 'Morning. Where's Lorenzini?'

'Upstairs, sir, typing a report. Somebody's just reported a 500 missing from the car park here. Shall I call him?'

'Never mind . . . I'm going out.' On second thoughts he said, 'I'll call him myself.'

He went to the foot of the stairs and shouted: 'Oh! Lorenzini!'

'Yessir!' Lorenzini clattered down.

'I want you to go back to the Pensione Giottino.'

'Keep an eye on that woman again, sir?' He began rolling his sleeves down.

'Exactly. At eleven-thirty she'll be going to a funeral at Santo Spirito. I'll be at the church, so once she arrives there I'll take over. I can't see her going anywhere before that but just keep watch, in case.'

'Right, sir.'

'Where's Di Nuccio?'

'Upstairs, sir.'

'Tell him not to go out until you get back.' He lowered his voice: 'I don't want Gino left in on his own; he's too young . . .'

As he went out, the Marshal rumpled Gino's chrysanthemum head and said, 'Take care, lad, I'll keep in touch with you.'

'Yes, sir. Will you be back for lunch, Marshal?'

'I don't know. I'll tell you when I phone . . .' Sometimes, on his day off he lunched at the NCO's club, but he had no thought of going there today.

The sun's blaze seemed more intense than ever since the rain had cleared the air yesterday. Heat shimmered from the roofs of the cars and coaches outside the palace, and swarms of Japanese tourists, always the earliest on the move, were pouring in through the main entrance. The postcard-seller was already doing a brisk trade and the ice-cream cart had just arrived. The Marshal made his way down the slope between the cars and went into a bar on the corner of the next piazza for some breakfast. The guard from the bank across the way was leaning on the ice-cream fridge in the doorway. He spent most of his morning there, sheltering from the heat, staring across at the bank and frequently dipping into the fridge where he kept his bottle of mineral water.

'Isn't it your day off?' asked the barman, when the Marshal ordered his breakfast and picked up a bar of chocolate from the counter display. 'How come you're in uniform?'

'I'm going to a funeral at Santo Spirito.'

'Ah,' said the barman. 'That must be the Dutchman, am I right? The one who committed suicide.'

Which didn't improve the Marshal's temper.

The Lieutenant was waiting for him when he reached the piazza and he quickened his pace a little.

'That's all right, Marshal; I got here a little early. Not that I'm expecting anything to happen, but even so . . . I thought perhaps we'd call in on the goldsmith since we're here, just in case anything's cropped up.'

'Good idea, sir . . .' The Marshal was wanting a word with the goldsmith, himself.

The apprentice was seated in a dark corner of the studio, dressed in a dark suit that he had probably had since his First Communion, as the sleeves were too short for him. He got up as they entered.

'Signor Beppe's in the back,' he whispered, 'if you want me to fetch him.'

But Signor Beppe had heard them come in and he appeared immediately, coming forward to shake both their hands without a word.

The Dutchman had been laid out in the dark suit and tie he had brought with him. Someone had thought, since last night, to put white gloves on his damaged hands. A black rosary was wound about them. He looked altogether solid and Dutch as he lay there. It had been his eyes, dark and merry, that had been his mother's legacy, that and his talent for drawing and designing. The Marshal crossed himself, then beckoned to the goldsmith to follow them out of the room.

Outside the frosted glass door, after a glance at the Lieutenant for permission, the Marshal said:

'I'm sorry to bring this up on the day of the funeral, but we have very little time . . .'

The goldsmith followed the Marshal's words carefully, evidently puzzled at a sudden lack of friendliness in his tone.

'When you said Signora Goossens left here immediately after the funeral, did you mean that literally? The same day?'

'More like the same hour. She didn't even come back to the house, as far as I know, and nobody had seen her for three days before that, the three days during which the post-mortem took place because of its being a sudden death. She shut herself up in the flat and didn't want to see anyone. She must have been deeply upset.'

'Did you go to the funeral? You would have known if anything had happened, like a quarrel?'

'No, I wasn't there.'

'You weren't . . .' The Marshal stared at him and then at the Lieutenant who seemed as puzzled as the goldsmith as to where this was leading.

'Even so,' the goldsmith pointed out, 'I don't see who she could have quarrelled with; Toni was in Amsterdam.'

'Why?'

'Why? Well, he was working there then. He was courting his wife, too. And in any case, she didn't invite him to come, so . . . Excuse me a moment . . .'

A hearse had drawn up outside and the undertaker's men were getting out.

'I'll have to leave you a moment, they want to seal up the coffin and take it over to the church. This way,' he directed the men. 'In here.'

The Marshal took out a handkerchief and mopped his brow. 'I don't understand this at all . . .'

'I can't quite see what you're getting at . . .' The Lieutenant was cool and impeccable in his uniform; the Marshal, being out of temper, had already become overheated and was sweating profusely which, in this weather, was a disaster. There was no hope of cooling down again until he got the chance to take a cold shower.

'I'm trying to get at the reason why the Dutchman wasn't at his own father's funeral. If there was a quarrel, perhaps it occurred before old Goossens died. I also ought to tell you, sir, that I left someone off my list of people last night. It was stupid of me and I can only think it was because I'd had nothing to eat all day other than a sandwich.'

'I'm sorry, I should have seen you got a decent meal in the evening but there really wasn't time—but how is it you didn't eat at lunch-time?'

'Something cropped up,' said the Marshal crossly, mentally kicking himself. He couldn't go on like this . . . perhaps it would be better to come clean . . . but if it ended badly? And it was the Lieutenant's first case . . .

'Who was it? The person you forgot?'

'The sister. Signora Goossens had a sister who lived out here with her for a time and was, by all accounts, an unpleasant character, jealous and vicious. At least,' he corrected himself, 'according to Signora Giusti, she was. Nevertheless, it seems that Signora Goossens always helped her, and I'm wondering if they now live together in England, and if it was the sister who was here on Sunday night.'

'When the Dutchman was expecting his stepmother?'

'Exactly. That would be why he was surprised. And then along comes Signora Goossens, the virtuous, all surprised to find he's dead.'

'But why, Marshal? I'm afraid none of this will impress the Substitute Prosecutor, even as a theory. Why should this terrible pair murder the poor man?'

'To be honest, sir, I haven't the faintest idea, and what's more, I don't think we have much hope of ever finding out, even if we had a year to do it in, let alone a few hours. We're dealing with intelligent people, crafty people. What sort of hold does this Goossens woman have over the people round here that they all defend her, in spite of her vanishing, in spite of the way she looks! Family quarrels, sir. They're the very devil in families like this where everybody covers up for everybody else, even relations they hate, rather than have a scandal.'

'Perhaps,' said the Lieutenant, 'we should go up and see Signora Giusti. Time's getting on. We can at least find out the sister's name which will help us to try and find out when she arrived here and where she stayed. Even so, I'm afraid that we may be too late.'

'It's probably too late already. Signora Goossens may have stayed for the funeral but the sister will already have left.'

The coffin was being brought out and they moved up on to the staircase to let it by. As it was carried out into the blinding sunlight of the piazza by the goldsmith and his fellow workers, the shoppers and stallholders paused to cross themselves, and a group of young German holidaymakers in shorts stopped to stare. One of them took a photograph of this bit of local colour.

The Marshal climbed the staircase behind the Lieutenant.

At first, nobody answered their ring, and when, after a long wait, a harassed social worker opened the door, they could hear Signora Giusti wailing somewhere behind her. It wasn't the wheedling little sob that she could turn on and off at will, but a very different noise, a repetitive, rhythmic wail like that of a child lost or left alone too long.

'She fell out of bed,' explained the social worker, 'some time during the night. She's very distressed and she's hurt her wrist. What is it you want?'

'Could we see her for a moment?' the Lieutenant asked, glancing unhappily at the Marshal who had got him into this.

'You can if you like. It might bring her round a bit. I've put her back to bed . . .'

She opened the bedroom door for them.

'I'm going to make her a warm drink so that I can give her a sedative.'

The outer shutters of the bedroom were closed, and the sunlight made a striped pattern on the white counterpane and the bare floor.

'Signora Giusti,' whispered the Marshal, bending over her. But she didn't answer. The steady, rhythmic wail continued. It was more like an animal sound than a human one. It must have been going on for hours because her voice was hoarse. One frail hand lay outside the white cover with a bandage round the wrist. The Marshal was afraid to touch it with his own great hand. Instead, he whispered again:

'Signora Giusti, we've come to visit you . . .'

This time there was a slight break in the rhythm and she moved her head a little.

'We've come to visit you,' he repeated, not knowing what else to say.

'I really think we'd better leave,' murmured the Lieutenant unhappily.

But then the old lady seemed to notice them, and the eerie wailing modulated into a human sobbing.

'I fell out of bed,' she wept, 'and I've hurt myself; look at my poor hand, look at it . . .'

'I know,' said the Marshal softly, 'but you'll be all right now.'

'Have you come to see me?'

'Yes, we've come to see you.'

She didn't even ask if he'd brought her anything.

'I've brought you some chocolate,' the Marshal said, but she went on weeping, sometimes breaking into the inhuman wail again, sometimes crying like a child.

'I had to lie on the floor, all night on the floor . . . and I didn't know even what time it was . . . because it was dark . . . and I thought I was going to die . . . on my own . . . on the floor . . .'

'It's all over now . . .'

'I don't want to die on the floor . . .'

'You won't. You're not going to die. The Signora's bringing you a drink now, and then you'll have a good sleep.'

The young woman came in and lifted Signora Giusti's head to give her sips of warm milk and a tablet.

'Does she have sleeping pills?' asked the Marshal quietly.

'Good heavens, no. I should think a real sleeping pill would kill her; it's just a very light tranquillizer.' She tucked the old lady in. After a few moments the sobbing tailed off and stopped and the old lady was asleep. The bandaged hand still lay outside the coverlet.

She seemed much too small for the high, old-fashioned bed, her tiny face sunk into the huge pillows. Above her, the dusty mahogany cherub warned them to be silent. The three of them tiptoed out to the corridor.

'Will she be all right?' the Lieutenant asked. 'Shouldn't she have a doctor?'

'I don't think so,' said the young woman. 'It's only a little bruise on her hand. I put the bandage on to make her feel better.'

'What happened exactly?' the Marshal asked.

'She wet herself in the night,' answered the young woman with an embarrassed glance at the Lieutenant. 'It happens sometimes. She tried to get up and see to herself and she slipped. She ought to be somewhere where she's looked after all the time, but it's donkey work trying to get her to leave this house for a month during the summer, and we'll be very short-staffed before long with the holidays starting. I was hoping you might have persuaded her . . . she seems to think a lot of you.'

So the Marshal, too, had escaped her vicious tongue, like the Dutchman's family. He could feel the Lieutenant's eyes on him saying, 'And you wanted to accuse her . . .'

'I did what I could,' he said, 'but she's afraid of being robbed.'

He could have kicked himself, remembering that the social worker herself had been accused of fishing under the mattress.

The young woman picked up a bundle of wet bedlinen and a nylon nightdress from which all the colour had long since been washed away.

'If there's nothing further . . . I want to take these down to the laundrette while she's still asleep . . .'

The Marshal looked with innocent expectancy at the Lieutenant, who eventually forced himself to say, 'If I could just ask you one or two questions . . .'

A single bell was tolling out in the piazza and the Marshal, hearing it, mumbled vaguely, 'I'd better go down . . .'

He felt, rather than saw Lorenzini come into the church, trying not to clatter, managing, nevertheless, to knock over a pile of requiem mass leaflets from the end of the bench as he got in. They began whispering.

'Well? Did you keep her in sight?'

'Yes, all the time. But she did go out and I had to take a taxi. Will it be all right?' Meaning would he get the money back.

'Yes, of course.' The Marshal resigned himself to paying for it.

'Where did she go?'

'To the Palazzo Vecchio. I waited outside for a bit, since there's only one public entrance, then I decided to follow her in.'

'That was stupid of you; you could easily have lost her inside.'

The Palazzo Vecchio again. Then she must have had a real reason . . .

'I didn't lose her. I caught her coming out of the Registry.'

Why should she go there? Surely the Medico-Legal Institute would have registered the death, and if not, then Signor Beppe who organized the funeral . . . though she might have wanted a copy of the death certificate. Was that what she'd wanted yesterday? No wonder she was furious then! In trying to shake him off she had made herself too late. He remembered the office workers coming out as they arrived. Funny. She must surely have known they closed at twelve . . .

'You didn't find out what she'd asked for?'

The Registry was a long room where Kafka-like queues of people waited wearily for computer print-outs of their civil status, which they needed for everything, from applying for a passport to enrolling each year at school. There were always quarrels among the irritable queues, or at the desk where some unfortunate person, having waited two hours or so, would be told he hadn't brought the right documents with him to enable him to get the document he wanted. The Marshal could imagine Signora Goossens standing grimly in one of those queues with that tight-lipped, self-righteous look on her face. Perhaps it wasn't a certificate of the stepson's death that she wanted; it could well have been a copy of her marriage certificate or some other document relating to whatever happened years ago—her husband's death certificate?

'You didn't see which counter she came from?'

'No. I wanted to stay and ask but I would have lost her.'

'You did right.'

The small congregation sat down, and one or two people turned to wonder what all the whispering was about at the back. These included Signora Goossens who started visibly at the sight of the Marshal's familiar bulk. Had she thought she would be free of him after her visit to Headquarters in the role of the grieving relative? One person on the front row remained standing longer than the others; a woman very smartly dressed in black, her wavy hair a false pinkish blonde colour. It was sure to be the Dutchman's mother-in-law, a Protestant, ill-at-ease in a Catholic church. She always stood or knelt a little after the others, after a covert glance around her.

The Marshal looked briefly at his watch.

'Go back there, will you? To the Registry, I mean—you might just make it before they close. You'll have to run, it's a quarter to twelve already. Then go straight back to Pitti; I'll phone you there.'

Lorenzini tiptoed out, this time without knocking anything over, but pulling the great door closed behind him with a crash that echoed through the whole building.

It was criminal, the Marshal thought, slipping on his dark glasses as the funeral party emerged into the overpowering midday heat, to ask anyone to run anywhere in such weather, but a taxi would have been slower because of the amount of traffic and the one-way system, and the Registry only opened in the mornings and tomorrow would be too late.

There was some embarrassment over the cars. Signor Beppe had ordered two, one for the family and the other for himself and the people from his studio. The other goldsmiths and jewellers who had been invited were in their own cars. Signora Goossens and the Dutch mother-in-law had never met, so Signor Beppe had quietly to play the diplomat and persuade them into the first car together. They settled themselves at opposite sides of the back seat in silence. They looked very much alike from the back, the Marshal noticed, though the Englishwoman was much smaller.

'That would be the Dutch mother-in-law, I expect,' said a small voice at the Marshal's shoulder.

He turned. It was the blind flower-seller, standing with his face turned up, listening.

'I shan't go to the cemetery, of course, but I thought I'd come across and hear the service. The priest spoke very nicely, I thought.'

'Very,' agreed the Marshal, who had been too busy with Lorenzini to hear a word of the brief sermon.

'Of course, you were busy with other matters,' remarked the blind man blandly. 'Any news yet?'

'No . . . not really . . .'

The hearse was starting up its engine.

The blind man made the Marshal feel clumsy and un-observant, but now it seemed he wasn't quite so observant as all that, because he said:

'I was hoping Signora Goossens might have come over, to tell you the truth. Even in such sad circumstances, it would have been nice to have a little chat like in the old days. Still, it's a long journey, no doubt, from England, and perhaps nobody let her know . . .'

'We let her know all right.' The Marshal opened his car door. 'And she was in the first car with the mother-in-law. Perhaps she wasn't in the mood for chatting.'

'In the first car? Yes, there was another woman who got in before the mother-in-law . . .' He turned his pale face in the direction of the cars which were starting to move. 'But you're wrong, Marshal. It wasn't her.'

'For crying out loud!' raged the sweating Marshal, slamming his car door repeatedly and uselessly. The blind man was tapping his way slowly back between the market stalls to his alcove of flowers. The car door closed at last and he made off in pursuit of the funeral cortège, catching it up on the other side of the river. 'It's all deliberate, it must be! They're all going out of their way to confuse me. They must be hiding something. They must be in cahoots with those wretched women. And somebody must have something to gain from all this. They must have! Well, if it wasn't her, it was her sister, and if it wasn't her sister, it was her. We'll charge them both is what we'll do!'

He changed down as they began the steep climb up to Trespiano where, above the hospital city, the red and white radio masts stalked across the wooded hilltop against a dazzling deep blue sky. The slopes below were covered by the cemetery.

'Which one of them did it is almost irrelevant. For all I know they might have travelled on each other's passports. But I'll have them both!' His fist crashed down on the steering-wheel. 'By God, I'll have them both!'

They were at the cemetery gates.

When the Dutchman's coffin was being slid into the *loculo* beside that of his parents, the Marshal stood right behind Signora Goossens, breathing down her neck which was blotched with nervousness. The plaque commemorating old Goossens and his Italian wife had a little vase attached to the front of it containing a few long dead flowers. The Marshal wondered who had put them there. The woman didn't so much as glance at it. When the sealing of the *loculo* began, the Marshal slipped away to the administrative building and asked to use the telephone.

'Gino? Listen, I won't be back to lunch—has Lorenzini got back yet?'

'Not yet. Marshal, there's been a call for you from . . . wait . . . the Pensione Giulia. The proprietor wants a word with you. He seemed nervous.'

'So he should be.'

'Sir . . . ?'

'Nothing. He'll have to wait. He knows very well Thursday's my day off; he's probably just trying to annoy me. If he calls again, tell him I'll ring him when I get back.'

'When will that be, sir?'

'I haven't the faintest idea. Don't worry, I'll be in touch with you. I have to go now. Ciao, Ciccio.'

The red icon lamp had been lit on the front of the *loculo* and the funeral party was coming towards the office. The Marshal noted that it was Signor Beppe who handed in the print-out of the death certificate and a photograph. From these the inscription and ceramic picture would be made and put on the front of the Dutchman's place in the wall. Had Signora Goossens collected the death certificate for Signor Beppe? He could have asked her to do it when he phoned last night, but it seemed unlikely. It was essential to draw him aside as soon as possible and ask him.

The Marshal managed to waylay him as they came out of the main gates of the cemetery. Only the hearse had driven in; the other cars were parked in a gravelled lay-by outside on the slope.

'Was it you who collected that death certificate you've just handed in?'

'Of course. Yesterday. I arranged everything.' He made to get into the car.

'Wait . . . What did old Goossens die of?'

'Heart trouble. He died in hospital. Why? Is something

the matter? Excuse me, Marshal, but are you feeling all right? We were standing so long in the heat that I don't feel too brilliant myself . . .'

'No . . . no, I'm all right. Tell me, Signora Goossens and her sister . . . would you say they were alike, I mean that they looked alike?'

'I suppose so . . . yes; it's just that they were so different in character that one didn't remark it. Signora Goossens was a little bit plumper when she was living here—always blamed Italian food, fond as she was of it. Living in England she seems to have slimmed down again. She's not the cheerful soul she was in those days, but I suppose we're none of us getting any younger . . .'

Here we go again, thought the Marshal, mopping distractedly at his broiled neck. 'You're quite sure it is her, are you?' he asked aloud.

'*What?*'

'You're quite sure it's her? You don't think it might be her sister?'

Where was the blasted woman anyway? The first car was leaving with only the mother-in-law in it.

'I don't understand . . . her *sister?*'

'Yes, her sister!' A nameless idea was rising in his mind, and his gorge with it. Where was she . . . ?

'But of course it's not her sister! I don't see what you're getting at!'

That's why she hadn't known her way round Bobili all that well, why she hadn't known what time the Registry closed . . . but what a fool she had managed to make of him, even so! But the nameless idea was still at the back of his mind and he knew before it happened that Signor Beppe was going to confirm it.

'I'm getting at the sister,' he persisted. 'That's clear enough, isn't it?'

'No, it's not, not to me. I don't know what you mean, but I know that's not the sister, that it's Signora Goossens!

I know it for the same reason you know it!' Signor Beppe was red in the face. He looked at his workmen for support in this ridiculous situation. They were all peering up from the car, the driver, too.

'You've asked me about it enough times!' expostulated Signor Beppe. 'The woman's dead, for heaven's sake, she's been dead ten years! I told you that after the funeral Signora Goossens—'

'After *her* funeral? For God's sake! I thought you were talking about old Goossens's funeral!'

'But that was the year before. It was after that that Signora Goossens invited her sister out here and then the sister died—if it had been old Goossens's funeral I'd have been there, wouldn't I? And Toni would have been there . . . well, everybody round here knew the sister died . . .'

'Well, nobody told me! And ten years ago I wasn't here!'

He spun round on the gravel and ran heavily in through the gate, running the handkerchief round his neck as he went. They watched him for a few moments, baffled, until the driver said, 'Shall we go?'

'I suppose so.' Signor Beppe got into the car and it pulled away from the gates. All except the driver were craning their necks and shading their eyes to look back.

The Marshal's khaki-clad figure thumped along rapidly, sometimes churning up gravel, sometimes grass, as he sought short cuts. After a while he stopped, looking this way and that. The graves went on as far as the eye could see, miles of them. The place was deserted under the merciless midday sun. Not a bird or an insect broke the silence of death among the grassy humps and cracked jars of half-rotted flowers. The burning rays beat down upon the Marshal's back where a large patch of sweat had already soaked through his jacket. His breath was loud and painful.

'If I'm too late . . .'

He began to make for the administration building. As he came near he bellowed to the official who had let him telephone earlier. The man came out with a cigarette in his hand and pointed out the direction the Marshal wanted.

'He'll have a heart attack, if he doesn't watch it,' the man remarked to himself, tossing his cigarette into the gravel as he watched the Marshal thunder away. 'He'll not need to bother going home . . .'

When he had still some distance to go, the Marshal spotted the group of three he was looking for, but he didn't slow down until he was close enough to distinguish her face, until he knew she had seen him, until he saw she was terrified, too terrified to try to run away from the spot where the two men were busy about the opened grave.

The men only noticed him when they heard his panting breath, and then they paused in their work. He signed to them to carry on and they set about opening the coffin. The ossuary lay in wait beside it.

He kept his eyes fixed on hers. She was trembling a little and sweat was running in little runnels down each side of her powdered face. She might faint but she was going to stand her ground, staring defiantly back at the Marshal's black glasses. She was wearing a black dress and her chest rose and fell beneath it as if she, too, had run all the way there. The chinking of the workmen stopped, and they were both aware of the coffin's being open without looking down.

'Right, Signora .   . ?'

The men were waiting. The Marshal was determined not to look before she did. He wanted to see her face when she looked down into the coffin. She held out as long as she could, but the men showed signs of impatience; there was nothing she could do. Slowly, she lowered her gaze.

What had the Marshal expected to see on her face? Repentance? Grief? Perhaps just any sign of human feeling. He was disappointed. He saw her lips tighten and her chin withdraw in a little involuntary jerk as the familiar expression settled over her lined countenance.

I had the right . . .

'All right, Signora?'

She nodded, and they prepared to go on with their work.

The Marshal only took a brief look knowing what he would see.

Signora Goossens's bones were clean, apart from a little mummified skin. Her burial gown, though dark yellow, remained intact until the shovel picked up the first bones when it disintegrated. When one of the skeletal crossed hands fell sideways off the ribs the tiny diamonds, emeralds and sapphires reflected the brilliant sunshine from their bed of lacy gold.

He turned away a little as the remains were shovelled without ceremony into the small ossuary that would be sealed into a wall.

'God rest her soul,' he said to himself, seeing her, long ago, listening to the blind man's proverbs, to Signora Giusti's complaints, enjoying the blessing of her second life . . . He heard the woman interrupt the workmen and he knew what she was doing.

'And God forgive me for having unknowingly maligned her . . .'

'A relative?' asked one of the workmen sympathetically afterwards, seeing that he was moved.

'No . . . no . . .'

'It's usual to have the priest . . .' murmured the workman with a disapproving glance at the woman. She was wearing the ring.

The Marshal didn't follow them to see the ossuary sealed in. Instead, he waited in the office where, in due course, the woman would have to come and sign the register to confirm that the remains had been identified and permanently re-buried. She might panic and run away, but after what he had just seen, he doubted it.

'I need to use your phone again.' If he had wondered before why, after the Dutchman's death, she hadn't left her sister's bones to rot in a communal grave, now he knew. He was powerless to prevent the sealing going ahead or to unseal the ossuary, without a warrant.

Funerals, quarrels and diamonds. And all of this because the sister, apart from anything else, had been too mean to pay for what Signora Giusti called 'a respectable burial'. She mustn't have known what burial in the ground would mean; it mustn't be the custom where she came from. And nobody had enlightened her, everybody assumed she knew—naturally, since she was supposed to be Signora Goossens who had lived many years in Italy and had respectably buried her husband in that same cemetery. Who would have thought fit to comment on her decision? Who even knew about it, apart, that is, from Toni who must have been the one to come up here and put those flowers on his parents' *loculo*. He knew, and he was sure that his stepmother wasn't the sort to leave her sister's bones neglected when the ten years was up . . .

'Hello? Lieutenant Mori, please. I know he's in conference with the Substitute Prosecutor, it's about that that I'm ringing . . . he's expecting . . . yes, yes, and hurry up . . . Hello? Hello? Thank you. Lieutenant? Marshal Guarnaccia. I have to be quick; I'm still at the cemetery. I've found out everything, or more or less everything. That woman isn't Signora Goossens but her sister. Signora Goossens died ten years ago and the sister registered the death in her own name . . . yes . . . yes—I don't know except that between the death and the funeral she shut herself in the flat and refused to see anybody, and after the funeral she left without coming back to the flat. The stepson was in Amsterdam, anyway, and no one seems to have been invited to the funeral. She settled in England well away from where Signora Goossens had lived and sold the English house through her solicitors . . . well, all she had to do was imitate the signature, letters can be typed . . . in any case it seems they looked fairly alike, so . . . I know because of the ring which I think I mentioned to you yesterday, a unique piece which Signora Goossens always wore and which wouldn't come off once she put on weight. It was still on the body which I've just seen exhumed. The sister was too mean to pay for a *loculo* and obviously didn't realize what a free burial in the ground would entail—I don't know, maybe it's not the case in England . . . The point is that the re-burial order was sent on to Amsterdam when it arrived here . . . it's easy to see why, all the mail addressed to Goossens T. was left at the studio for Signor Beppe to deal with; after all those years it's not surprising that neither he nor the postman remarked on the letter from the Council being marked Sig.ra and not Sig.

'The Dutchman had been expecting something of the sort because he mentioned the possibility of his step-mother turning up now. There are flowers on his parents' grave, which suggests he came up here when he was in Florence and so knew about the sort of burial . . . yes, it would be only natural . . . exactly, it was his one chance of seeing her—and I wouldn't be surprised if, in sending the letter on he offered to see to the re-burial himself if she couldn't bring herself to do it, and that would have been the end, he would have seen the ring. At all events, he must have intended to come up here with her so she must have been desperate even before they actually met and he recognized her. She must have come out here quite prepared to—no, it's being sealed in, how could I stop them, we'll need a warrant . . . But there *is* evidence, the ring! All right, but surely he can take my word for it . . . !'

It was incredible! Surely, after all this they couldn't refuse . . .

'Yes. Yes, sir, I know you can only do your best — but there are witnesses; Signora Giusti . . .'

But Signora Giusti, the Lieutenant informed him, was still lying as they had left her except that there was now a nurse beside her. She had no specific injuries and she might well come round to her normal self at any time, it had happened before. But she also might not. If she lived there were plenty of witnesses to the fact that she was a chronic liar. An interview with the Substitute Prosecutor would be a heaven-sent opportunity for her to air her juiciest accusations.

The Marshal was beside himself.

'There's another witness! A neighbour who knew Signora Goossens for years! The blind flower-seller in the piazza — he'll swear this woman isn't her. All right, he's blind but . . . even so, he can still hear! He can still tell one person from another — yessir. Yessir. What should I do now? Very good, sir. I'll follow her as long as I can but if she leaves the country . . .'

If she left the country that was the end. If they hadn't enough evidence for a warrant now they could forget the whole thing. Impersonation wasn't an extraditable offence and they had nothing concrete on her as far as the murder was concerned.

He could see the woman approaching at a distance. It must be over. Quickly he dialled Pitti.

'I don't know who's supposed to be paying for all this,' grumbled the official. 'I'm supposed to pay for all my calls . . .'

The Marshal flung five hundred lire on the table and glowered at him.

'Gino? All right, lad?'

'Yes, sir. Lorenzini's been in and wanted to speak to you but he had to go out again. There are witnesses who saw that car being driven away this morning, a couple who happened to park their car right next to it just as it was being stolen. They've just come back and, when he saw what time they'd parked there, the attendant asked them to wait and came to tell us. Lorenzini's out there now getting a statement. He's left a message here, though, in case you rang—shall I read it out?'

'Never mind, it doesn't matter.'

'But, Marshal, Lorenzini said it was vital, that you needed to know urgently . . .' There was disappointment in Gino's voice.

'I know, but I've already found out. It was the death certificate of Theresa Goossens . . .'

'No, that's not the name—'

'That's right. . .of course it's not. . .what is her name?'

'Lewis.' He had difficulty pronouncing it. 'Joyce Lewis.'

'All right.' What sort of mentality did you have to register your own death like that? 'There's nothing else?'

'Only . . . the man from the Pensione Giulia phoned again. He was furious.'

'Oh, was he? And why was that?'

'Because . . .' Gino was embarrassed at having to repeat it. 'Because he says you're always round there pestering him—that's what he said, Marshal—'

'All right. Go on.'

'But that when he needs you you don't show up. If he rings again—'

'If he rings again tell him to call 113!' growled the Marshal.

The proprietor of the Pensione Giulia did ring again, speaking in a furious whisper:

'You get round here or I'll report you! Do you hear? I'm a respectable citizen and I have a right to help when I need it. All you lot ever think about is harassing people! But I'll have you fired! I know people in this town, I'm a personal friend of . . .'

Gino, who had never even heard of the influential people the man claimed as his friends, didn't know what to do. If somebody with influence tried to get him fired would the Marshal be able to stop him? He thought so. On the other hand, he'd heard of cases, not of people being fired, but of their being suddenly transferred. He had to stay in Florence with his brother. They had never been separated . . .

The phone rang again.

'Is somebody coming or not?'

'I . . . yes . . . someone will come . . .' Perhaps Di Nuccio would . . .

'Well, make it quick, I'm telling you! This is serious!'

'I think you should phone Headquarters then, and they'll send a patrol car round . . .'

'I'm phoning you, aren't I? Because you're two minutes away. If I have to phone your Headquarters you'll be sorry.'

The respectable citizen didn't say that he didn't fancy having any trouble-shooters from Headquarters nosing around his place; the Marshal was a pest but there was a bit of give and take. Better the devil you know . . .

Gino put the phone down. Perhaps Di Nuccio . . .

Di Nuccio, still in his sullen and uncommunicative phase, was upstairs typing with the fan placed on the desk beside him and his shirt open to the waist.

From the top of the stairs Gino said:

'There's this man from the Pensione Giulia keeps ringing up wanting one of us to go round there . . .'

'Tell the Marshal when he rings,' mumbled Di Nuccio without looking up from his work.

'I did. He said tell him to ring 113.'

'Well then.'

Gino waited but Di Nuccio went on typing without saying anything further. It was hopeless trying to talk to him this week.

'We need some mineral water,' he ventured timidly. 'That's the last bottle you've got there. Somebody will have to go to the bar . . .'

'Damn! Now you've made me make a mistake!' Di Nuccio had no real desire to trouble with getting himself smartened up to go out and get broiled. He typed a noisy row of X's irritably over his mistake.

'If you'll listen for the phone until Lorenzini comes in,' Gino said, 'I'll go.'

'The Substitute Prosecutor wasn't pleased, I can tell you . . . we haven't told the Consul yet so he must be wondering what these interruptions are all about. We'll have to tell him and the mother-in-law, I suppose, before they leave. Anything further at your end?'

What more do they expect? wondered the Marshal, but he said: 'No, except that she gets more and more frightened . . .'

They were in a tourist self-service restaurant and he had her in view from the cashier's desk where he was telephoning. She had selected an unappetizing array of brightly-coloured food and was sitting with it untouched before her, taking occasional sips of water with a trembling hand.

'She's so keyed up that if I moved in on her now she'd crack completely.'

'There's little chance of that, I'm afraid. We haven't been able to get in touch with the Instructing Judge who may or may not have signed the *Archiviazione*. It seems he's on an express train on his way up from Rome.'

'Then surely he won't have signed, since it was to be done after the funeral . . . It's something, anyway, if the Substitute Prosecutor wants to get in touch with him. At least that means—'

'It means he's covering himself against all eventualities.

Nevertheless, he doesn't altogether disbelieve your story.'

Good of him, thought the Marshal.

The woman still wasn't eating and one or two of the other customers had begun to stare at her. He was aware that on his right holidaymakers were streaming noisily past the window where, on a refrigerated stainless-steel shelf, rows of stemmed glass dishes held identical blobs of imitation ice-cream topped with bright red strawberries.

'He pointed out, of course . . . are you still there, Marshal?'

'Yes.'

'He pointed out that we still have nothing concrete, that Signora Goossens could have given this ring you mentioned to her sister.'

'Except that she couldn't get it off, if you remember.'

'That's something that would be pretty impossible to prove at this stage. In any case, as a piece of evidence it doesn't weigh very heavily against the woman's embarkation card — you hadn't forgotten about that?'

It was true that he had ceased to think about it. But if there were no longer two suspects and this woman had only entered the country on Tuesday, the day after the Dutchman's death . . .

'There's no chance of there being any mistake?'

'Hardly. We all know what the French customs and immigration are like . . . in any case I saw her ticket which was for that date.'

'I see.'

'You don't think,' the Lieutenant suggested hopefully, 'that she might have an accomplice, a man perhaps, whom we know nothing about?'

'No . . .' The Marshal looked across at her; she was dabbing shakily at her mouth with a handkerchief. 'No, I'd say she was a loner.'

'Well, there it is then. I've got someone checking on where the Dutchman bought his food — I was able to persuade the social worker to let me borrow a photograph from Signora Giusti's album. I take it you've ceased to suspect the old lady?'

'Yes.'

'Well, we'll do what we can . . .'

There was something about that 'we' that included officers and magistrates only; the Marshal very much feared he had lost his only ally. He put through a call to Pitti next, staring straight at the woman as he did it. She was only a hairsbreadth from collapse but her iron hard selfishness was keeping her going even as her frightened eyes watched his every move. He was her enemy. She couldn't know that he was powerless to touch her and no doubt she imagined that his phone calls concerned traps he was setting for her all over the city. Had she been able to hear them she would have been baffled.

'Gino? Oh, it's you, Di Nuccio. Has Lorenzini come in?'

'Yes, he's only just started his lunch. Shall I call him?'

'There's no need. Just tell him to stand by, I may need him again. Where's Gino, anyway?'

'He went for the water.'

It was very hot. The streets were empty when Gino walked down Via Mazzetta towards Piazza Santo Spirito after dropping off the empties at the bar on the corner. He would collect the full water bottles on his way back. He had decided that he would call at the Pensione Giulia just to keep the proprietor quiet, and if there really was a problem he would ring Headquarters himself. That way, he thought, he would be suiting everybody. The Marshal hadn't meant it about 113, he had only said that because he was in a temper about something. Anyway, he'd had to come out for the water so it was only common sense, whichever way anyone looked at it . . .

The proprietor was waiting anxiously behind the door upstairs.

'You took your time! This way, they're in room ten.'

'Wait,' Gino said, for though he knew very little of the world he had learnt from the Marshal to be cautious. 'Tell me first what's going on.'

The man looked nervously towards the corridor that led to the bedrooms and said in an undertone:

'There are two rum characters holed up in there that I don't like the look of at all, and I'm sure that at least one of them is armed. I got a glimpse of a holster . . .

'Listen . . . two youngsters booked into that room last night. They arrived late on the train from Rome. Nice kids, well-dressed, good-looking . . . and plenty of money . . . I could see that right away. The room's booked for two nights. After they'd gone out this morning, these two rum characters turned up. They gave me a fright, I can tell you.'

'Why?'

'Why? Well, just their attitude. They started off asking for the young couple, polite enough, but when I said they were out but were expected back before lunch, they looked at each other, funny-like, and went off muttering in the corner over there. Eventually, they said they'd wait. They insisted on waiting in the room itself and since I have no sitting-room . . . well, I didn't like to refuse. I found them a bit sinister, you know what I mean? I called you right away, you know, so if anything happens . . .

'They've been in there ever since . . . they insisted I didn't say anything to the couple when they came in, that they wanted it to be a surprise. Well, I know from experience what that sort of surprise means . . .'

'You do?'

'In a manner of speaking.' The respectable citizen pulled up sharply. 'The things I've read in the papers . . .'

'And what happened when the young couple came back, or did they?' Gino was copying all this carefully into his notebook.

'Well, I warned them, didn't I? I don't want anything

nasty happening on my premises. They left straight away.'

'What time was that?'

He calculated. 'Just over an hour ago. That's when I started calling you again . . . if those two come out they're going to start on me, aren't they?'

'This couple: they left without their luggage and without offering any explanation as to who the two men might be?'

'Well, they'll be back, of course.' He sounded a little less sure of his ground now. 'They haven't even paid me. I watched them go from the window there. They got into their little car and drove off round the block.'

'Just over an hour ago.' Gino looked at his watch. 'What time did they leave the first time?'

'Early-ish . . . I suppose just after eight.'

At half past a car was stolen at Pitti.

'You said before they came on the train.' Check all the ordinary details, the Marshal always said.

'So they did . . . Well, maybe they borrowed a car . . . I never thought . . . What are you going to do?'

'Ring Headquarters.' What else would the Marshal do? 'And look at your blue register.'

'Lieutenant? It's me. Any news?'

'Nothing. Someone will meet the Ambrosiano express when it gets in from Rome and collect the Magistrate. Where are you now?'

'Back at the Pensione Giottino where she's staying. She's in her room, supposedly taking a nap.'

But she wasn't asleep. The Marshal, to the manager's fury, had gone up to the next floor and knelt down unashamedly to look through the keyhole. She was sitting rigidly on the edge of the bed, staring straight ahead and wringing a small handkerchief between her thin, claw-like hands.

'There's not much I can do unless the Substitute Prosecutor decides . . .' The Lieutenant sounded nerveracked. Was he wishing he'd never got into this?

The Marshal persisted. 'You said you saw her train ticket; what made her show it to you?'

'I think I'd told her that the funeral was Thursday and she said she thought her booking on the return journey was for Wednesday. She got it out to check and I took the opportunity . . .'

'The opportunity she was offering you, sir,' finished the Marshal as politely as he could. Why couldn't there have been an experienced man on the job! 'I don't know how often there's a flight to England, but if she took one on Monday, could she not have got there in time to get the train back and arrive here on Tuesday?'

'I'm not sure . . .'

The Marshal waited patiently.

'I'll speak to the Substitute Prosecutor; if he agrees we could start checking. It would take time, of course . . .'

'And we haven't got any. Even so . . .'

'I'll do what I can. In the meantime, if you want to get home, I could try and get him to send someone . . .'

But the Marshal had to stick it out to the end, even if she won. It was no longer a matter of choice. He had no willpower to do anything other than doggedly follow this woman who filled him with horror, plodding after her until some outside force separated them.

'No,' he said, 'I'll go on waiting here.'

CHAPTER 10

Gino made one last phone call.

'Di Nuccio? It's Gino . . . at the Pensione Giulia, since I was passing . . . Listen, can you check two names for me against the list?'

There was no need to say which list. He read the names out from the blue register.

'They are? Thought to be in Rome, that's what I remembered seeing. Yes, here, or they were . . . nothing yet except to call Headquarters, and in any case they've got away, but there are two men here who will be the agents who are following them . . . No, I won't, except to tell them that they got away in a 500 — yes, it must be because that would be about the time that they stole it, so if you'll give me the number . . . right . . . yes, I've got that. I'll tell them straight away so they can get after it, and then I'll wait here for the men from Headquarters and explain. Right, see you later.'

Gino tore the bit of paper from the telephone pad where he had scribbled the car number.

'Show me to the room quickly!'

Sirens could be heard faintly in the distance.

'None of this is my fault,' cried the proprietor, now thoroughly frightened. 'I called you right away. I'm covered.'

The two of them ran along the squalid strip of carpet that led to room number ten. The sirens were getting louder.

The two Digos agents who had been waiting tensely for two hours inside the room heard the frantic wail of the sirens and the two sets of running footsteps at the same time. The couple they were following had six killings to their names and were known, on occasion, to use sub-machine-guns. The first agent had fired two shots before the door burst open. The other fired a split second later. By the time they saw Gino there was a small red hole like a third eye between the two mildly surprised blue ones.

'Bloody young fool!' screamed one of the agents at Gino as he fell back and cracked his blond head against the door jamb. '*Bloody young fool*!'

The other, terrified out of his senses, was still firing uselessly against the wall.

The Marshal's last call came from the station at ten minutes past two. The woman had appeared suddenly at the pensione reception desk, her face covered in red blotches but her expression determined. He knew, even before she had ordered the taxi, that she was going to try and leave, defying him to stop her. When the receptionist had tried and failed to get her a seat on the afternoon flight she had asked for a taxi to take her to the station. The ticket she had shown the Lieutenant, although it had a couchette booking for Wednesday, was valid for three months.

'It's me, Guarnaccia. We're at the station. She's leaving.'

'What time?'

'Now, more or less. Does it matter now, anyway?'

'It might. We've found that she flew in to Pisa last Sunday. There isn't a flight out after the time the Dutchman was killed so she couldn't have left again until Monday morning at the earliest, which means she must have flown back to get to London in time to take the train she did. It also means she must have stayed somewhere on Sunday night. We're checking every possible place, but we're largely dependent on luck now, on hitting the right place early on. The Magistrate's train gets in at thirteen minutes past two. What time's her train?'

'In about twenty minutes.'

'I see. That makes it seem pretty hopeless. I'll go on with it, anyway. There's always the chance that her train might be late.'

'It already is late, curse it.'

That was just the trouble. He had followed her to the station where she had gone to try and change the booking for her couchette.

'Booking's closed for that train, I'm sorry. It's been taken off the computer. In any case, couchettes for Calais were booked up two days ago, so . . .'

If the woman had made a fuss or lost her temper, the clerk would probably have started serving someone else and ignored her, but she stood there staring at him, paralysed. Having got herself this far, she was evidently incapable of re-thinking or even of turning back. Sensing this, the clerk felt obliged to say something.

'Do you want me to check tomorrow night's train?'

She stared at him uncertainly. Taking her silence for assent, he tapped out the code and waited for a printed card to come out of the machine. When it did, he said: 'That's booked up, too. I'm sorry, Signora.'

Still she stood there, unable to take her eyes off him, willing him to get her on to a train. He scratched his head, staring down at the card.

'Can't you stay another day or so?' he asked, wanting to cheer her up a bit. 'Don't you like Florence? Stay with us a bit longer and I'll see when I can get you a couchette . . . weekend's difficult but Monday's often quieter . . . what do you say?' He even, recognizing her accent, tried to ask her in English: 'You like Florence? A beautiful city? A few days more, eh?'

The Marshal was standing to one side of the ticket window, a few feet away from her. He saw a bead of sweat break on her temple and trickle down towards her neck. The queue behind had begun to take an interest in the case and now a white-suited man pushed his way to the front to offer advice.

'Surely, if it's a matter of an emergency, the Signora could travel without a couchette.'

'That's true,' put in a woman, 'I've done it myself and it's not all that bad. Only as far as Paris, mind you, but even so . . .'

'Not on this train,' the clerk tutted and wagged his finger. 'Couchettes only. There are no ordinary seats. It's always possible that someone may cancel, of course, but I can't help you there. It means waiting until the train comes in and speaking to the *chef-du-train* . . . if you want, though, I can check the Amsterdam carriage, there were a couple of places on that when I last — what's the matter? Don't look so frightened, I'm not trying to pack you off to Holland! All the carriages travel together as far as Thionville, in France; you could change to an ordinary carriage when they re-make the train tomorrow morning.'

'Poor thing, look at her, she doesn't look fit to cope . . .'

'Travelling gets worse every year . . .'

'She's in black, too; I think she must be bereaved . . .'

'What's the problem?' Another railway official had come up to his colleague behind the window. 'Here. Someone will collect this ticket at three. I'm going off. What's the hold-up here?'

'This Signora wants to take the Holland express, the nineteen-forty-one this evening, but the couchettes for Calais are booked up.'

'Well, her ticket's valid three months; she must go when it's not booked up.'

'I know, but it's the same tomorrow night, and . . .' He indicated the woman's black garb and blotchy white face, so incongruous among all the healthy brown limbs and light summer clothes.

'Just a minute.' The second clerk hurried out of the booking-office and reappeared in seconds with a solution.

'Express two hundred, the thirteen-twenty-seven Holland-Italian — no couchettes on it at this end but she'll get a seat and couchettes will be added further north. She'll have to change in Milan.'

'But surely, it's gone . . . ?'

'Should have done. Travelling seventy minutes late. It hasn't got here yet . . .'

The Marshal had been obliged to lose sight of her while he telephoned, not that it mattered now. After hanging up he made his way slowly through the crowds and potted palms to the board showing the composition and departure platforms of the principal trains.

'Thirteen-twenty-seven . . . platform ten . . . let's hope it's at this end . . . no . . . Basilea . . . Amsterdam . . . baggage . . . Oberhausen . . . here we are . . . Milan but first class . . . second . . . seven carriages and probably half a mile to walk . . .'

But still he didn't ask himself whether he was wasting his time.

As he plodded along the platform to its furthest point, he thought rather that the Lieutenant seemed to have undergone another change of heart and was hot for the chase again, which was odd.

The Marshal wasn't to know that, quite by chance, a young journalist, hanging around Headquarters on the look-out for a story, had spotted the Dutch Consul coming out of the Substitute Prosecutor's office and recognized him. With a bit of effort he had uncovered the whole story.

'It's got everything,' he had told his editor excitedly on the telephone. 'Family row, priceless heirloom, mistaken identity, ten-year-old mystery unravelled . . .'

Already the headlines were being prepared for tomorrow:

MYSTERY DEATH OF INTERNATIONAL DIAMOND MERCHANT! FAMILY SECRET BURIED WITH CORPSE!

The journalist and one or two of his colleagues had rushed to the cemetery, the goldsmith's home, and back to the Carabinieri Headquarters where they cornered the Substitute Prosecutor and the Lieutenant. The Substitute Prosecutor had practically snatched the Goossens file from the Lieutenant's hand.

'We've been investigating this for some days now, naturally . . .'

'And you have a lead?'

'Let's say we have a number of indications, all of which we are checking on very carefully.'

'Do you expect to make an arrest? What's to stop this woman leaving the country?'

'Up to now, I'm afraid, nothing.'

And since they knew there wasn't a train until seven-forty-one in the evening, they had all dashed off to the airport in Pisa.

'Express two hundred, the thirteen-twenty-seven from Rome, for Basle, Lucerne, Frankfurt, Paris, Brussels, Amsterdam and Calais is about to arrive at platform eleven, travelling seventy minutes late . . .'

The Marshal was no longer alone. The Magistrate's clerk who was waiting for the Ambrosiano to arrive from Rome spotted him and came across to ask if he was there for the same reason. Then the Magistrate himself arrived and the three of them were together on platform eleven when the Holland Express pulled in. The *Archiviazione* had not been signed.

As they talked, all three of them continually glanced down the platform, wondering if at any minute a warrant would arrive.

The woman got into the train.

The platform was suddenly alive with trucks of newspapers, sandwiches and drinks, and a motor was coming along pulling a long baggage train. There was a huge stack of post to be taken on board; it would be some time yet before the train left. People got in and out or wandered along the corridors, blocking them with cumbersome luggage. A girl came up and asked the Marshal in German: 'The carriage for Oberhausen?' thinking, perhaps, that he was some sort of railway official.

He indicated the label saying Milano and pointed. 'Further back.'

In the operations room at Headquarters, the Lieutenant was pacing up and down nervously. Every now and then he would stop at one of the switchboards and say: 'Nothing yet?'

'Nothing. Do you want me to try places out in the suburbs?'

'I don't think so . . . Wait! I wonder if she would have dared try and use her own old passport? Not for the journey but in some not too particular hotel . . . It would be out of date, since she had been officially "dead" for ten years and she would hardly have dared try and renew it even had there been time, which was hardly possible. She had had so little warning of the reburial. Try it! Because if she registered under a false name on Sunday night we've got her — and if she decides to claim it as her real name then we've got her for registering at the Giottino under a false one!'

They began to check under Simmons, the married name of Signora Goossens's sister, elicited from the gold-smith an hour earlier. If they could arrest her for a false registration they would have time to investigate the whole case. It was the one thing that would help them.

The Marshal had the piece of information they wanted in his top pocket, but he didn't know they were looking for it, and he didn't know the married name of the woman. He only knew her as Joyce Lewis, as mispronounced to him over the telephone by Gino. All Italian official documents are made out in a woman's maiden name.

The passengers were now shut into the train and many of them were hanging out of the windows, reaching down to try and touch the hands of those who were seeing them off. The baggage truck was trundling away and the food trolley was already out of sight down near the ticket barrier. The train was so long that it took three guards signalling in relays, each with a sharp blast on his whistle and his green sign held aloft, to start it. It slid backwards out of the station, almost noiselessly at first. The Marshal's last glimpse of the woman showed her sitting erect and still very tense, staring straight ahead of her, but, as if hypnotized by his intense gaze, she couldn't prevent herself from a rapid glance in his direction, and he saw the beginnings of a look of triumph in her frightened eyes.

The train picked up speed noisily as the carriages rolled interminably by. Most of it was out of sight round a distant bend by the time the last of the passengers, the ones in the carriages going to Amsterdam and Basilea, began to shout and wave.

The Magistrate and his clerk offered the Marshal a lift. He thanked them and said he would rather walk. He was so tired he would have to send Lorenzini for his car.

It was over, then, and he felt nothing except weariness and relief. His only desire was to get back to his Station, to his lads, to his own world. He had been struggling like a fish out of water, trying to cope with people he didn't understand and with work for which he had neither the brains nor the training. Well, he had brought it on himself so there was no point in trying to blame anybody else.

He no longer knew or cared whether he had been right or wrong in his suspicions.

What made him look up as he crossed the river? He had forgotten all about the young Count. Nevertheless, there he was at the first-floor window, looking out hopefully. No doubt the pale face had been there yesterday afternoon, too, as promised. But the Marshal was too exhausted to bother with him. Perhaps tomorrow . . .

He trudged down Via Maggio and was about to cut through to the left when he remembered the calls from

the Pensione Giulia. He could ring when he got back to
the Station, of course, but it might be better to call there
now, so that once he got home he could sink into a chair
and fo.get everybody. After all, this was supposed to be
his free day! He crossed to the right of Via Maggio and
carried on walking. The road was quiet in the heat, the
shops still closed. Not a soul observed the heavy, plodding
figure as it made its way slowly along the narrow pavement, or when it stopped, and after a quick consultation
with a small black notebook, moved on again, its pace
quicker and more purposeful than before.

'Stand back, please! *Stand back*! Do you want to come
through, Marshal? Stand back! There's nothing to see.
This way, Marshal . . .'

'What's happened?'

The whole of one side of the littered piazza was
crowded with jostling onlookers. There were a lot of
official cars and police cars, and an ambulance with its
doors open.

The carabiniere on duty outside the Pensione Giulia
looked disturbed. He was very pale.

'You don't know? But I thought it was one of your
boys . . . Didn't they send for you?'

But the Marshal was already running up the stairs.

The crowd inside the Pensione seemed worse than outside, although everyone was there on official business.
The Prefect was there, talking rapidly in an undertone to
someone the Marshal had never seen before. Photo-
graphers and technicians were pushing their way towards
the reception hall from along a narrow corridor, holding
their equipment above their heads to facilitate their
passage. The Marshal began to push along in the opposite
direction. Nobody noticed him; nobody spoke to him.

The noise in room ten was deafening. There were a lot
of uniformed men, all officers. The two Digos agents were

still there, and one of them, white in the face, was sitting on the edge of a bed with a small glass in his hand. The proprietor was moving from group to group, expostulating to anyone who would listen:

'I hope you realize! I'm covered! Whatever happens . . .'

The only space was near the doorway where Gino's body lay covered with a grey blanket, blocking the entrance. A little of his untidy corn-coloured hair was visible, protruding from the blanket. With so much noise and movement in the room no one was paying any attention to the shape under the blanket, except for a tall, fair boy in uniform who stood beside it with his hands over his ears as if he couldn't bear to hear the words he was groaning, hoarsely and repeatedly, above all the other voices around him.

'It's my brother . . . It's my brother. . . It's my brother!'

An officer tried to lead him away, but the boy shook him off and then grabbed him by the lapels and screamed right into his face:

'*It's my brother!*'

CHAPTER 11

The silence closed in around the Marshal. He had switched on the living-room light and was sunk deep in his armchair, but the light was unaccountably gloomy and the silence seemed to be pressing down from above where no sound came from Di Nuccio and Lorenzini. Perhaps he ought to go up and see them but he couldn't face it. Were they, too, sitting listening to the silence that used to be filled by Gino's radio?

The Marshal had carried the radio, along with Gino's other personal belongings, over to the school. The brother was in the infirmary under sedation. When he recovered sufficiently he would make the train journey back to Pordenone and on to his own village along with the body. Another boy would be sent with him to stay and take care of him until he was well enough to come back to school, if he came back at all. It was pointless to send a boy home on compassionate leave if it was only going to cause a hard-pressed family extra work and expense, and isolate the boy from friends who were in a position to understand.

Gino's little bundle of property didn't amount to much when the Marshal placed it on the Adjutant's desk. To the Adjutant, the Marshal had felt he could unburden himself a little.

'I'm trying to understand,' he had said. 'I'm trying . . . but all these scandals we keep hearing about . . . politicians and such-like who, it seems, have been cheating us for years . . . between them and these spoilt brats who think they know all the answers and are too clever to care about killing off a few of us lesser mortals to get what they want . . . well, what I'm asking myself is, where does a lad like Gino come in? Why should he be the one? You didn't know him . . . he wasn't clever or ambitious . . . but he was a good lad . . .'

And he had tailed off lamely and sat looking down at his big hands.

'He was a carabiniere,' the Adjutant said gently. 'He did his best. He's not the first to be killed on duty and he won't be the last.'

It wasn't what the Marshal meant at all, but he had neither the intellect nor the words to explain what he felt was all wrong. It had nothing to do with dying on duty, nothing to do with 'Faithful through the centuries'. It was to do with the Ginos of this world always being the ones to pay, no matter what they were trying to do. But since he couldn't explain, he said: 'Yes, Major . . .'

'There'll be a formal enquiry, of course, you realize

that? There's no question but that they were in the wrong.'

Agents of Digos, the secret police, had no right to operate in an area without informing the local forces. It had happened all too often that citizens in some public place had phoned for the police or the carabinieri on seeing some apparently respectable people removed at gunpoint from their meal or film. The resulting embarrassing situation left the local forces feeling foolish and enraged, quite apart from the danger involved.

'They can't go on acting as though they were a law unto themselves,' the Adjutant want on. 'I also wanted to tell you that, although in this case it ended in tragedy, I do know that the control you keep over the hotels in your area is appreciated. It's often been so useful . . . well, we hope you won't abandon it because of this . . .'

The Marshal stared at him with feverish eyes.

'You don't understand,' he said slowly, 'you don't understand that even though it might have been useful in other ways . . . you see, it was just to avoid *this* that I did it.'

Now it was eight o'clock in the evening. He couldn't make up his mind to eat anything. He hadn't showered or changed out of his sweaty uniform. He wouldn't go into the kitchen and turn on the television because he didn't want to see the eight o'clock news. So he went on sitting there, sunk in his chair, his mind rambling.

It was the telephone that roused him from his stupor. He answered it in the office.

'Is that you, Marshal?'

'Who's speaking?'

'It's *me*!'

'And who's me?' He wasn't in the mood for this sort of thing.

'Me! Signora Giusti!'

'Signora! But I thought . . .'

'I know! You thought I was always in bed by half past seven—well, I am, but not tonight. I've got things to do!'

'I thought,' he said cautiously, 'that you'd hurt your hand . . .'

'I have. I've got a bandage on it—if you'd seen me this morning . . . people don't understand what it means to fall at my age . . .'

She interrupted herself for a little weep, then sniffed and carried on:

'I've decided you were wrong.'

'I was . . .'

'You're fussing over nothing—of course it's your job, I realize that. Anyway, in spite of all you said I've decided to go. After all, I've gone every year up to now and nothing's ever happened. I can't see any point in my sitting here all summer while everybody else goes on holiday, on the off-chance that I might get robbed.'

'No . . .'

'Oh no. I'm not saying that caution isn't a good thing. I said as much to the woman from the Council, I said he's only doing his job, but he's exaggerating, and she agreed. I hope you won't take offence?'

'No, Signora, no . . .'

'That's all right, then. This is what I want you to do: they're collecting me on Monday morning some time after ten, so I want you to come round here between nine and ten and I'll give you my keys. That way I shan't have to worry because you'll be able to keep an eye on things, pop in and so on when you're passing.'

'But I—'

'Don't touch anything, mind!'

'I—'

'I'll be able to phone you now and again from up there. And I'll send you a postcard—there's a little shop and a bar. It's not a hospital, you know, more of a holiday home. It's very select. They can't take many people but

I'm a special case.'

'Yes, I realize that. Well . . . I'm sure you'll enjoy it.'

'I will. You're sure you're not offended?'

'No, no! Heavens above . . .'

'Good. You see, it's wicked of me, I know, but I do like to have my own way.' She chuckled and rang off.

Within seconds the phone rang again.

'It's me again—I forgot to say—her ladyship from downstairs came up to tell me about your arresting that woman I heard in the flat next door. You can tell me all about it when you come round. Good night!'

'Good night.'

He sat down in his chair. It was very hot in the little office.

Ten to nine. He should at least get changed. Goodness knew what garbled stories were going round the piazza, or who had started them. She hadn't even mentioned the Dutchman, as if she had forgotten him already. Her emotional reactions were as short-lived as those of a child. Was it just selfishness? Or was it just because she was ninety-one? Nothing seemed to touch her because nothing could affect her life, which was over. How could he blame her if her chief concern was her funeral . . .

Again the phone broke his reverie.

'Surely not a third time!'

But it was Lieutenant Mori.

'You've heard, of course. Whoever would have thought it? And we're officially having to start a completely new investigation because the Instructing Judge signed the *Archiviazione* as soon as he reached his office! I've been on the phone to Chiasso for almost an hour—I thought you'd want to be up to date, since you've been in on it from the start. It seems to me a good idea if you could—'

'I'm sorry, sir,' the Marshal was obliged to interrupt him, 'but I don't understand what it is that's happened '

'You don't . . . ? But . . . didn't you see the eight o'clock news?'

'No . . . no, I didn't . . .'

'It was nothing more than a flash, of course, the full story isn't out yet. The main thing is that she attacked a Brigadier on the train!'

'She *what*?'

'Nobody knows why she did it. It's a complete mystery. There were other passengers in the carriage and they all say the same: no apparent reason for it at all. The man hadn't looked at her, spoken to her or even seen her. Of course, it all happened very quickly . . .

'It seems that when the train drew into Chiasso it was stationary rather more than the usual ten minutes or so. A carabiniere squad got into the train to do a spot check on passengers and luggage . . . ever since the Red Brigades kidnapped that train we've been doing it fairly frequently, especially in the north.

'According to the witnesses, they hadn't even reached the Calais carriage, but one of them, this Brigadier, came ahead and was standing outside their compartment talking to the *chef-du-train* with his back to them. The woman seemed suddenly to lose her wits. She got up, wrenched the door open and set about the unfortunate Brigadier with her fists, beating him frantically on the back and screaming at him hysterically. You can imagine how astonished he was! At any rate, she didn't do him much harm; he's a biggish chap, apparently, something your build. Nevertheless, he took it rather badly, he said he'd never seen such virulent hatred on a face in all his life—on top of which she smashed a new pair of sunglasses that he happened to have been holding behind his back when she leaped on him. Nobody's managed to get to the bottom of what started it all . . .'

The Marshal shuddered. Certainly the attack was meant for him. Did she think he'd got on the train? If she had relaxed, thinking it was all over, it wasn't surprising that her nerves gave way when she saw that broad expanse of khaki on the horizon once again.

'I suppose she denied everything?'

'Not a bit of it! The only trouble was getting an interpreter over to the station-master's office as fast as possible so that we could get it all down. She does speak some Italian but mostly she was giving vent to her feelings in English. Far from denying anything she kept on insisting that she was in the right . . . they all thought she was crazy—in fact they were pretty sure that she was inventing the whole story. She may be crazy, anyway, of course, to do a thing like that. After all . . . she told her story expecting sympathy!

'It happened, more or less, just as you thought. The sister died of a stroke ten years ago. The two of them were alone in the house at the time; the stepson was up in Amsterdam. It seems that, although the death occurred at seven in the evening, the ambulance wasn't called until late next morning. She claimed at the time that they had gone to bed early and slept late and that she had found her sister dead in bed. Since there was no doubt, after the post-mortem that the cause of death was a stroke, I suppose nobody thought anything of it. In fact, she must have sat alone with the body all night, thinking out her plan. Don't you think she might really be mad?'

'She's mad that we've caught her,' murmured the Marshal. He had an old-fashioned belief in the human capacity for good and evil which no psychiatrist's report had ever managed to dislodge.

'If you'd heard what they told me . . . the way she screeched at everyone present. *I had the right to do what I did. I had the right to a bit of happiness in my life. Eleven years I nursed a sick husband who was no good, who left me penniless after all I'd done for him! Who cheated me out of his life insurance with an overdose of sleeping pills just to spite me. While* she *had everything.'*

She had even accused her sister of being responsible for old Goossens's death.

'It's her you ought to be investigating, not me. Ask her if her husband wouldn't be alive today if she hadn't insisted on their doing so much travelling about. His heart wouldn't stand it, I always said so, but her ladyship would have her holidays and he was fool enough to give her everything she asked for. I've been nowhere, do you know that?

'Some of the time she talked about her sister as though she were still alive. You can imagine why they didn't believe her story at first. Nevertheless, she insisted on telling it, saying every so often, *I had a right to something after the years I suffered. She left everything to him, everything! And he was supposed to go on providing for me. As if he would bother. Men are all alike, I've learned my lesson. He was no better than the rest, too busy chasing some woman up there to bother about me.*

'This was the Dutchman, I suppose . . .'

'Yes, poor man,' said the Marshal, 'and he would have provided for her even if he hadn't been asked . . .'

He shuddered to think of that night when he must have embraced her, thinking she was his stepmother. It was surely one of her hairs they'd found on his jacket. How long would it have been before he realized? Not very long, according to Signora Giusti's account of when the row broke out. But by then he must have drunk the coffee. What had made him realize? No doubt he had noticed that she wasn't wearing the ring, for one thing . . .

'Are you still there, Marshal?'

'Yes, I'm still here.'

The Lieutenant sounded a little disappointed at his lack of enthusiasm, but it all seemed so far away after what had happened to Gino.

'What isn't clear, up to now, is what went wrong. She

left the country the following day and arrived back here on Tuesday. She could have seen to the re-burial on Wednesday and left again without taking the risk of appearing at the Dutchman's funeral. And that must have been her intention because we've checked with the cemetery and she had made an appointment for Wednesday and was told to present herself with a copy of the death certificate from the Council, but it seems that she didn't turn up, and later she made a second appointment for after the funeral on Thursday. But nobody knows exactly why, much less why she came to see me . . .'

It was more than likely, the Marshal thought, that she had been trying to get into the flat when he'd first spotted her because there was a copy of the death certificate there, but he had unknowingly blocked her way.

Then he had unknowingly prevented her from getting to the Palazzo Vecchio before the Council offices closed so that she'd had to wait a day, and so she had been forced to turn up at the funeral.

Then he had turned up at the re-burial and seen the ring.

She had certainly seemed to have some bad luck. Nobody had explained to her what burial in the ground entailed, assuming that it was something everyone knew. And nobody had noticed that the letter from the Council to Goossens T. was for once marked Sig.ra instead of Sig., so that the postman had left it with Signor Beppe and Signor Beppe had sent it on to Amsterdam where the Dutchman had been hoping for just such an opportunity for a happy reunion. A lot of bad luck. Nevertheless, she'd had ten years of living her sister's life, of spending her sister's money.

Sooner or later, he would have to explain everything to the Lieutenant, but not now . . . he couldn't cope now . . .

'Are you all right, Marshal?'

'Yes . . . I'm all right.'

'I'm sorry . . . I wasn't thinking . . . It was one of your boys, wasn't it?'

'One of my boys, yes, sir.'

'I hadn't forgotten. I just thought that you'd like to know . . . well, that you were right.'

'Yes, sir. Thank you, sir.'

'I shall need you tomorrow. We're going on checking the hotels where we left off. We think she may have used her old passport in a not-too-fussy hotel—she must have stayed somewhere on Sunday night.'

'Was her married name really Simmons?'

'Yes. Maiden name Lewis, married name Simmons—why? Do you think you can help?'

'She stayed at the Pensione Giulia. Her passport number was on the register but not the date of issue. I was going to check up on it this afternoon, but then . . .'

When the Lieutenant rang off, the Marshal found he was feeling a little more in possession of himself. Probably it was just because he had talked to somebody, filled the silence for a while. It wasn't that he felt any better for having been right. He didn't feel any more 'right' now than he had before. He only felt lonelier.

Even so, he persuaded himself that he must have a shower. Once in his pyjamas, he was convinced that he felt perfectly normal and was coping well.

In fact, he had left the lights on in the office. He had quite forgotten that he had eaten nothing. He had also forgotten something else.

The telephone started ringing again.

'Whoever can it be this time?' He went back into the office in his pyjamas, and was surprised to find the lights on.

'Yes?'

'Salva! Whatever's happened? I've been waiting almost an hour!'

It was Thursday. He hadn't telephoned his wife, who must have been waiting at the priest's house all this time.

'Teresa . . . I'm sorry . . .' How could be begin to explain? 'Didn't you watch the news?'

'No, of course not, I was on my way here. You haven't had an accident? Salva!'

'No, no, I'm all right. It's one of my boys . . .'

When he had told her, she said: 'You mustn't blame yourself.'

'Of course not,' he lied. But he was thinking, If I'd only been here . . .

To distract him, she said, 'The boys are getting so excited . . . they want to buy a new beach ball . . .'

'I'll bring them one . . . Listen, about Mamma.' The holidays had brought Signora Giusti to mind. 'If you think this hospital idea is a good one . . . well, you're the one who does all the work, and you need a rest . . .'

'Oh, but you made me forget! With this terrible business about the boy . . . Nunziata went to see the boss after I'd told her you were against the hospital idea—there was nothing he could do, of course, because everybody's holidays were fixed. Anyway, she got in a bit of a state and I think she was crying—well, after all, she'd been promised. Anyway, while she was there a woman came into the office wanting time off straight away instead of in August. Just fancy! A woman whose child had to go into hospital. It's an ill wind . . . Well, with Nunziata being there what could he do but give her the August fortnight . . . So, you see, you were right. It was best to wait like you said.'

Why did being told that once again he was right serve to depress him even more? For some reason he was thinking of the newborn baby that must be lying in one of those painted metal cribs in a hospital somewhere in Amsterdam. Would he inherit his father's talent? What difference could it possibly make to his tragic start in life

that an obscure Italian policeman had been right about
what happened to his father? The Marshal could feel that
he was transmitting his depression to his wife. To distract
her, he gave her as brief an account as he could of the
Dutchman's story, the ring, the vicious sister. It sounded
not only remote but outlandish when he summarized it.
But it did the trick; his wife was intrigued.

'You'll tell me all the details when you come home?'

'Of course, if it interests you. You'll probably see it in
the papers before then . . .'

'I think it's fascinating. Especially about the ring . . .
and the way these people travel about . . . they must have
money . . . and talent too, just imagine. What an interesting
family!'

'I suppose so.'

But it all seemed so far away.

'Didn't you find them fascinating? After all, it's not
often that you have to deal with a business like that.'

He thought again of the baby in its crib, of the Italo-
Dutch boy in his black artisan's smock weeping at the
kitchen table and his father standing over him, big and
helpless, of Signora Goossens sitting among the blind
man's flowers and reminiscing about her English garden,
of a woman looking down into a coffin without flinching,
a blonde girl with her dog in a Dutch garden . . . and her
mother who was perhaps already travelling north on the
Holland Express . . .

'I suppose you're right,' he said at last. 'They are a
fascinating family, it's just that, well,' he finished lamely,
'I never spoke to any of them . . . I think we'd better say
good night, now.'

And because he could never manage to say anything
endearing over the telephone, he said:

'Sleep well.'

For a complete list of books available from Penguin in the United States, write to Dept. DG, Penguin Books, 299 Murray Hill Parkway, East Rutherford, New Jersey 07073.